BORDER GRAZE

To Ross Kincaid, trouble was an old, old friend with a familiar voice. And when he rode into Apache, that voice was loud and clear. When the price was right, Kincaid always welcomed trouble. But if he had known what he was getting into in Apache, he would have upped the price. But then it was too late. Ross found himself trapped between two factions—both after him with murderous hate—and he was fighting for his life with two roaring, bucking six-guns. But he refused to run.

BORDER GRAZE

Dwight Bennett Newton

First published in the United States 1952
By Doubleday and Company, Inc

This hardback edition 1997
By Chivers Press
By arrangement with
Golden West Literary Agency

*All of the characters in this book are fictitious and any
resemblance to actual persons, living or dead, purely
coincidental.*

ISBN 0 7540 8006 4

British Library Cataloguing in Publication Data available

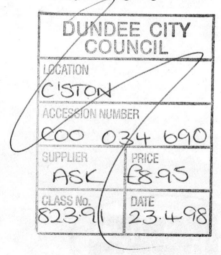
Printed and bound in Great Britain by
Redwood Books, Trowbridge, Wiltshire

CONTENTS

I   STRANGER IN TOWN

To Kincaid, any new town was a challenge—an unread riddle which might hold meaning for him, or on the other hand might count for nothing more than a meal or two, an evening wasted, a few faces seen but at once forgotten. Generally the interest lay in not knowing ahead of time what awaited him as he rode into some cattle center or lumber town or silver camp, in a region that was new to him.

But in Apache, though she might wear an unfamiliar face, he knew already the name of the siren who had lured him here. She was an old, old friend, and her name was Trouble. . . .

He rode into the place on the first waves of darkness that flowed across this sun-seared land from the skirts of barren adobe hills. He came out of the north; the trail he'd been following through this day's blistering heat wandered into a straggle of mud-and-mesquite-pole structures, and the liquid music of Latin voices ran upon the early night. Further along, past the squalor of the poorer section, the road widened slightly into a plaza of mean proportions; and about this center, with lamplight spilling from doors and windows, stood the business houses of Apache.

Ross Kincaid looked the town over, assaying it with a sure and experienced eye. Just another cow-country hub, like a dozen or more he'd passed through in his trek to this remote range. His business would take him farther yet tonight; but first there were questions to be asked, and meanwhile the belly behind his jeans' waistband was sucked in with emptiness. The dusty grulla mare, too, deserved a graining after the long miles. So he turned toward the wide doorway of a public livery standing opposite the old dobe mission that held its cross to the pale evening sky.

A lantern burned on a nail above the barn entrance, putting a spray of yellow light across the hoof-pocked dust and the splintered ramp. Its glow fell directly upon Kincaid as he leaned far out of the saddle so his long length could clear the low doorframe. He knew the light shaped him up to make a perfect target; however, it was a purely reflexive action that brought him quickly down, to place the grulla between him and the dark street outside.

There was really small chance that an enemy would be out there watching him.

No barn attendant was in evidence. He took care of the horse himself, putting it into one of the half dozen stalls, stripping off gear and saddle and sweaty blanket, and dumping feed into the manger. Afterward he had left the building and was halfway across the plaza on his way to the big, square hotel building when it occurred to him there was something in his blanket roll that he would need. So he turned back, retracing his steps to get it.

And, moving noiselessly across the straw that littered the barn's dirt floor, he came to the grulla's stall to catch a man hard at work pawing through his belongings.

Kincaid halted, his eyes gone narrow behind dusty lashes, his hollowed-out cheeks edged with bunched muscle, his thin mouth long and hard. The searcher did not look like the kind of stable bum he might ordinarily have expected to find hunting something to pawn for the price of a drink. This man was well enough dressed, in range clothing and good, solid cowhides and a hat that evidenced even less wear than Kincaid's own low-crowned, wide-brimmed sodbuster.

Rusty hair showed beneath the hat, at the back of his head, which was the most Kincaid could see of him. He was working industriously, making little animal grunts of haste. And all at once he let out a louder exclamation and, satisfied, drew back holding in his hand the very envelope Kincaid had returned for.

He was looking at the strong scrawl forming Ross Kincaid's name and that of a town two states distant when Kincaid remarked softly, "You see your name anywhere on that envelope, friend?"

The man jerked about as though he had been prodded with something red-hot and very sharp. Kincaid saw scared

eyes, a narrow face, and a red mustache that drooped over
a mouth hung wide with shock. Consternation shaped that
face with a dozen fleeting, half-realized expressions before
the man could squeeze out a few croaking sounds intended
to answer the quiet question. "No! No, I——"

Kincaid hit him.

His knuckles struck the slack lips, and the man went
back, slipping on the straw; fell on his side against the edge
of the grulla's stall. He lay there blinking and making no
move to pick himself up again. With those scared eyes on
him, Kincaid leaned and got the envelope that had tumbled
from the other man's fingers.

"Where I come from," he observed in a voice as emo-
tionless as before, "we don't count it polite to go through
another gent's belongings. Or to read his mail. Could be,
of course, around here they look at things differently."

He stuffed the envelope into a pocket of his shirt, his cold
gaze thoughtfully considering the one he had felled. Then,
leaving it at that, he turned on his heel and went out again
through the barn and into the soft night darkness.

He could hardly help wondering a little.

Someone must have noticed him ride in, he supposed,
and seen enough to rouse curiosity. Perhaps they'd even
recognized him—it wasn't entirely out of the question, despite his being a stranger to this corner of the range. Perhaps it was known that Kincaid was expected, and the redhead had been set to head him off and was checking first
to be sure of his man. . . .

He shook his head, dismissing these speculations, and
walked across the dust of the plaza to the hotel.

There were separate entrances to bar and lobby. Kincaid
chose the former; a drink would be a welcome first item on
his agenda, to lay some of the daylong accumulation of
dust that fogged his throat. A bar, too, was a convenient
place to gather information.

This one was not doing much business at the moment. As
he eased through the swinging half doors, Kincaid gave the
place a thorough, knowing scrutiny, with an eye that was
well enough practiced to tell from a single glance what the
whiskey here would probably taste like and how much it

would cost him. He saw a dingy, low-ceilinged room. There were a few cigarette-scarred gaming tables, deserted now; the bar had a mirror behind it that held a radiating pattern of cracks, like a spider web. Kerosene lamps in wall brackets gave the room a murky kind of light.

At the near end of the bar a single customer nursed a shot glass of whiskey. Kincaid had a feeling that this post had been chosen because it gave the man a view through the inner door that led off the lobby beyond; he looked as though he might be waiting for someone to appear there. He turned now and favored the newcomer with a sharp, black-eyed stare, letting his glance slide down Kincaid's dusty length to touch on the gun handle that jutted from a low-cut, half-breed holster snug against the lean thigh. Kincaid, for his own part, merely satisfied himself that the man was no one he knew and then walked toward the bar, a spur chiming.

The bartender was a round-faced man with a black mustache and thinning hair that he wore pasted in a stiff curlicue above his forehead. He asked sourly, "What'll it be?"

"Beer."

While this was drawn and collared, Kincaid drew out the envelope he'd taken off the redhead and had another look at the letter inside, checking again the signature of the man he wanted to find. He refolded the sheet of paper and was stuffing it back into the envelope when he heard the man at the end of the bar saying, "You just hit this town, friend?"

Kincaid flicked him with a look that was hardly an answer and reached for his beer. It tasted flat and warm, but wet. He drank slowly, letting the stuff work at the dust that stung his throat.

"Not many strangers come through Apache," the man observed. "We're kind of off the main trails, you might say —from here they lead nowhere much but . . . yonder."

A jerk of his solid head indicated the southern horizon and the distant hills, which would be entirely obliterated by this time, in the settling night. Kincaid knew what he meant. He was implying that Mexico lay over that way, and that it was a trail only a man of dubious purpose would be riding.

"Could be," said Kincaid indifferently, without com-
mitment.

The man wasn't to be cold-shouldered, however. He
edged nearer along the bar, slipping a pair of slender black
cigars from a pocket of his waistcoat, one of which he offered the stranger. When Kincaid merely shook his head,
hardly glancing at the weed, the man returned it to his
pocket and shoved the other between thick, meaty lips.
He had a heavy, squared-off jaw. His nose looked as though
it had been broken a couple of times, and his sharp black
eyes crowded the base of it.

"What I was goin' to say," he pursued, "being out of the
way as we are, it ain't always easy for a cattleman to pick
up men for his crew whenever he needs them. I mean by
that, good men—naturally. Now, you look like a good man.
If it should be you'd like a job, I'll pay eighty to start."
He added, "Britt Larkin's the name; the brand is Leaning 7."

"Eighty a month?" Kincaid echoed, passing up the intro-
duction. "That's almost gun wages."

The man's lips quirked; his sharp eyes again rested upon
the stranger's holster, briefly. "Don't you figure you could
earn 'em?"

"Maybe I've already got a job," said Kincaid merely to
be rid of him.

The effect of this on Larkin was startling. The eyes narrowed; the big head jutted forward; the mouth lost its smile.
"Hey! Don't tell me that skunk, Mayes, has already been at
you?"

"No, Larkin, I haven't," said a voice. "Still, maybe it ain't
too late to get into the bidding."

The pair at the bar turned. Just within the street door
stood the redhead from the livery barn. He looked a little
wild. His mouth was bloody where Kincaid had hit him,
and the handkerchief in his hand was bloody too. Mayes
dabbed it at a cut lip and added loudly, "I'll offer you a
hundred, Kincaid."

"Ross Kincaid?" Larkin swung a look of even greater interest at the stranger. His voice rimmed with a sudden note
of respect. "I guess maybe you could be him, at that! In

that case, the eighty I spoke of would be chicken feed! Let's make it a hundred twenty-five, friend?"

"One-fifty!" snapped Mayes promptly.

"Damn you!" The Leaning 7 owner whirled on his rival and the stain of dark blood showed, flowing up into the back of the pillarlike neck, reaching clear to his eyes.

"I tell you," he shouted, "I'll kill you myself before I let you hire this man out from under my nose, to use him against me!"

His voice bounced off the crowding walls of the narrow barroom; it echoed through the open door to the hotel lobby and out through the batwings into the plaza. In the general stillness of early evening it must have traveled far.

For a moment no one moved. Larkin stood at a half crouch, his head thrust forward, his eyes on the bloody face of the man named Mayes. Behind the counter the bartender had a towel and a tumbler in his hands, forgotten, and sweat was a greasy smear across his gaping features.

Then Ross Kincaid heard movement over by the lobby entrance and glanced that way quickly. The man he saw was not young; he had shaggy, grizzled hair and the hanging jowls and sagging eye pouches of an old mastiff. A noticeable potbelly pushed out the waistband of his trousers; and, visible in the gap of the hung-open black suit coat, a spear of light struck from the metal badge pinned haphazardly to his vest front.

This improbable figure, then, represented the law in Apache; but though quick violence seemed to hang upon the stillness of the room, the sheriff made no move to interfere in it. He stayed where he was, observing the scene with lackluster mastiff eyes.

It was Kincaid himself who put an end to this dangerous bidding for his services by turning and throwing a question at the scared man behind the bar.

"I'm here to look for a man named Ward Sullivan," he announced. "Could you tell me how to find his ranch?"

He might as well have lit a big, black bomb and tossed it into the middle of the floor. The effect couldn't have been more galvanic; even the sheriff looked jarred, his sleepy-lidded eyes widening considerably. The redhead,

Mayes, released his caught breath in a bubbling explosion of sound. The bartender, under the prod of Kincaid's stare, was the first to find his tongue.

"Why, sure, mister," he stammered. "You take the south road. There's a signpost at the crossing. Look for Block S."

"Thanks." Kincaid had dug silver from his pocket, and he tossed it onto the bar's zinc top in payment for his beer; the metallic sound appeared to jar Britt Larkin loose from the grip of whatever emotion had hold of him.

"You don't want anything to do with Sullivan!"

Ross Kincaid turned on him a cool, impersonal stare. "Mind if I be the judge of that?"

"But—but the man's a crook! Everyone knows that jailbird's Block S is no more than a blind for stolen cattle crossing into Mexico!"

Almost purple now, Britt Larkin had one thick fist clamped on the edge of the bar, the cigar tight in the other one. Ross Kincaid watched a purplish vein throbbing in his temple and thought: Better watch that blood pressure! But not speaking, he merely favored the angry ranch owner with a brief stare and then, moving around him, walked through the doorway that separated the bar from the lobby of the hotel proper.

He left dead silence behind him; and the fat sheriff drew aside to let him pass. Across the lobby, beyond a second archway, he saw the white-covered tables of a dining room. It should do as well as any. The desk was vacant, so Kincaid turned back to the sheriff and asked in a mild tone, "They got a place a man can soak the dust off him before he eats?"

The red-rimmed, mastiff eyes blinked; the hanging jowls stirred and shifted their folds. Finally, when Kincaid had almost decided the sheriff wasn't going to answer, a deep rumble of sound rose from the depths of the potbelly.

"Out back," said the lawman, nodding ponderously toward a corridor that split the building from front to rear. "A wash bench."

"Thanks," said Kincaid, and turned in that direction.

He found the battered tin basin and a pump; also a community towel which was crusted over stiff in spots. By such light as filtered through the screen door at the end of the hallway, he worked the pump handle and, setting his hat on the end of the bench, proceeded to splash water over himself.

It felt good, cutting through the alkali that lay in the creases of his skin. A beginning of coolness was in the early night too; the stars were all out by now, spangling the deep sky.

As Kincaid used the towel gingerly, the light from the door was blotted out, and he looked to see the shapeless form of the sheriff silhouetted against the opening. The man stood watching while he finished his toilet and picked up his hat from the bench, slapped the dust from it. Then the flabby jowls stirred, and again the rumble began inside and became speech.

"They tell me you're this Ross Kincaid."

"Why, yeah, I'm this one," the stranger admitted. "The only one I ever heard of, as a matter of fact."

The sheriff grunted sourly, "Ha, ha!" and went on in the same tired rumble: "Kincaid, you got you a reputation that's reached clear down here to this forsaken end of nowhere. You're dangerous to monkey with, and you know it; what's more, we know it too. But just the same, even for you it ain't smart flying in the face of public opinion!"

"Meaning Ward Sullivan?" Kincaid's voice was crisp now, all the banter gone from it.

"Meaning him! Gawd knows that rustler has given us trouble enough; but if he's gonna start importing hired gun hawks and bringing them in here to make a real ruckus——"

"What about Mayes and that big-talking Britt Larkin hiring gun haws? You were in there—you heard them bidding against each other, both trying to buy me. Doesn't that worry you any?"

The sheriff's shoulders lifted a little. "Hell! Charlie and Britt are just having a little personal squabble. Dunno what the bone is, but it won't come to anything—they're both solid, respectable gents. Not like that crook, Sullivan!"

"You're the law," Kincaid pointed out. "If Sullivan's a crook, why don't you do something about him?"

"Don't think I wouldn't," retorted the sheriff, "if I had the proof!"

"Oh." Kincaid shrugged. "And I suppose you figure to dig up proof by hanging around a hotel. Seems to me all you're accomplishing right now is to hold a starving man away from his supper. . . . Would you mind?"

His hand was on the knob of the screen door, and he jerked it open. For a moment he thought the fat lawman was going to continue arguing, but at the last moment he pulled back a little and made room to squeeze past. Kincaid nodded curtly, said, "Thanks, pardner."

The sheriff's mastiff face was dark with anger. He let the other go by him in silence; Kincaid retraced his steps down the long hallway to the lobby without looking back, and passed under the tasseled arch into the dining room of the hotel.

It was, fortunately, in better condition than the bar, but just as empty. He ordered a steak and, waiting for his food, leaned back in the chair, which he had chosen so as to face both the archway and the outside door, and rolled a cigarette.

He was tonguing down the flap when the girl appeared in the lobby entrance. For a moment he stared at her frankly above his motionless hands.

II   SHADOW SHOT

She was that kind of a girl. Especially in the drab, improbable surrounding of a cow-town hotel, a man was bound to look at her and look again.

Tall, well shaped, with a pile of soft, dark curls setting off a complexion that seemed hardly possible in such a land, she was dressed in a style and taste to match anything he had seen in a city as large and as far away as Denver. She had dark eyes and finely modeled features and a spoiled mouth. And she was frowning with irritation because she looked for someone she apparently didn't find.

Kincaid stuck the cigarette into his mouth, fumbled a match from shirt pocket, and snapped it explosively against a thumbnail. The sharp leaping to life of the flame brought her glance to him, and for a long moment their eyes met, boldly.

He thought there was interest in the cool regard she gave him, but then her eyes roved on, still searching through the room, and Kincaid casually touched the match flame to his cigarette and shook out the curled black stick, dropped it into a thick china saucer.

Britt Larkin came hurrying through the archway. The dark-haired girl turned to meet him, and, remembering how Larkin had been waiting at the bar in a position to watch the coming and going of people in the lobby, Kincaid suddenly realized these two must have had a rendezvous. But, for all his careful vigil, the big man had ended by missing it.

The woman seemed angry about this; Larkin had one huge paw laid up her arm and was talking quickly, placating her. Now he steered her into the room toward one of the empty tables. With a shrug and a pout of her red, full mouth she gave in and went with him.

At that moment the slattern waitress brought Kincaid his plate of underdone beef and watery potatoes and strong black coffee, and he was hungry enough to let other matters go while he tied into the food. He was used to this kind of grub, and to worse. He went after it with nearly as much relish as if the stuff had been halfway decent eating; and when his plate was empty and his cup drained, he settled back with a grunt of satisfaction and once more dragged out the makings—for an after-dinner smoke, this time. And his thoughts were on the girl again.

He knew a curiosity about her. He would have liked to know who she was and what business she had in a town which made so unsuitable a backdrop for her. Above all, he wondered what relationship could exist between her and a rough-handed, uncouth man of the type of Britt Larkin. In Apache, Larkin might hold some importance; but the girl did not belong in Apache. Money had been spent on her— you could tell that. She had known a larger world than this

sun-blistered, backward border town . . . and in that world,
Britt Larkin would have rated as a boor.

Kincaid watched the man working at his supper. Knife
and fork engulfed in massive hands, he hacked at his plate
of beef, punctuating his talk with gestures and shoving his
mouth full without interrupting the flow of words. Obviously he was wound up on some subject, and the woman
let him talk, saying little herself. Kincaid could watch her
face in profile, and he saw no expression. She hardly even
seemed to be listening.

She had small appetite, apparently, for the soggy food
and ate little, but Larkin cleaned his plate and mopped it
up with bread and let the waitress bring him a second cup
of coffee and a heavy slab of pie. The woman refused des-
sert, and her plate was almost untouched when Larkin
finally finished and they both rose. As they moved toward
the lobby archway, Kincaid snubbed out his second cigarette. He got up to follow leisurely, leaving silver on the
table with his bill.

The pair were only a few paces ahead of him when he
entered the lobby. At the sound of Kincaid's spurs, the
Leaning 7 owner threw a look across his shoulder—and
froze for an instant, big hand tightening on the arm of his
companion. She, too, looked around; for the second time
her eyes met Kincaid's.

Blue eyes, he saw now . . . as near to the color of violets
as he had ever known a pair of eyes to be. They had cool
depths, and their look was cool as they turned full upon
the stranger, meeting his stare openly and with a frank interest. His mouth quirked into the beginning of a smile,
and his glance moved to Britt Larkin's scowling, battered
face.

But the man turned his back sharply and, changing direction, steered the woman toward the room clerk's desk,
where a thin-haired old man was now on duty. Kincaid felt
a touch of amusement at this subterfuge.

Larkin, he thought, was really upset.

He ran a last, appreciative glance over the trim shape of
the woman at Larkin's side and then headed for the door

himself, pulling on the flat-topped, wide-brimmed black hat
he had been carrying in his hand. He stepped outside, beneath the mesquite-pole arcade that fronted the hotel building: and, turning in the direction of the livery barn, he had
taken perhaps a half dozen steps when a six-gun laid its
startling report across the stillness of the plaza.

The bullet kicked a stinging spray of dust from the
adobe wall, mere inches from Ross Kincaid's figure. But
even before he heard the thud of it striking home he was
hurling himself flat upon the hard-packed ground, moved
by an instinct that long acquaintance with danger had
drilled into him. At the same instant his gun had leaped
into his hand; he lay there searching for a target through
the shadows that shrouded the dusty square.

"Irene! No——"

The voice of Britt Larkin shouted frantic warning from
the hotel doorway, without result. For now light, running
footsteps were nearing, and someone leaned above Kincaid.
He felt hands pulling at him, felt breath warm against his
cheek.

Twisting, he looked up into the face of the woman.
Lamplight from a nearby window limned it dimly; her lips
were parted, her eyes a wide, dark stain. He heard her quick
breathing.

Kincaid grunted harshly, "Get down, will you?" And
when she failed to obey him he cursed and, reaching, seized
her about the waist and flung her prone against the dust.
Afterward, because he couldn't stay where he was and perhaps risk drawing fire to her, he came quickly to hands and
knees and leaped across her body, moving out into the plaza
at a running crouch with his six-shooter leveled and ready
to meet another shot from the ambusher.

All about the plaza, doors were opening, voices calling
excited questions in Mexican and English. But there was
no second bullet. Somewhere across the open square of
rutted dirt he thought he heard a quick scuff of running
footsteps, but they ended abruptly. He bore toward this
sound, himself running lightly now.

Directly ahead, the square bulk of the mission lifted its

cross to the night sky. The old wooden doors were tight closed, the dobe face of the building softened by the star glow. Ross Kincaid rounded a corner of the square structure and halted, shoulders against the rough, earthen wall as he listened and probed the shadows. He heard nothing, saw no movement.

Nevertheless, he started along the side of the building, for it seemed to him certain that the ambusher had taken refuge somewhere in that dense blackness. As he prowled forward his sleeve brushed against rough adobe; suddenly it touched wood, and he hesitated an instant, struck by a thought that left its traces as he moved on.

He reached the rear corner, then, and halted, every nerve stretched hard as he tested the quality of the utter stillness before him. An open space lay behind the old mission, a low adobe wall enclosing a small garden, where a few vegetables were tended by the padre and his helpers; beyond stood a well, and then a row of squat adobe huts with dim candlelight outlining the low doorways.

Over all was the quiet sheen of starlight, in which outlines were vague and unfamiliar. Detecting no near sound other than the calling of distant voices, Ross Kincaid knew an unreasoned conviction that his man was not here. There were places, true enough—behind the garden wall, perhaps —where he could be hiding with tight-held six-gun ready for a second try. Yet a certain intangible feeling for such situations as this, built in him by dangerous years, told Kincaid otherwise.

This feeling was so strong, indeed, that he now stepped boldly forward into the starlight and in a few strides covered the space to the well. He placed one hand upon the ancient well sweep, and, with the other palming his gun, paused for a long, full look about him.

There was still no movement, no sound. Unless the ambusher had already fled, there remained but one further place to look for him. . . .

Purposefully Kincaid heeled about and retraced his steps to that small door in the dark wall of the church. It was not set flush, and as his hand found the latch he distinctly heard, through the narrow crack below the door, a small stirring of sound. With a quick thrust he swung the door wide.

It opened almost silently, on heavy rawhide hinges. A suffused candle glow greeted him; taut nerves made the gun in his hand leap forward as he glimpsed a dim figure just within the opening. But he quickly caught himself and lowered the weapon with a grunt.

The man was small and stocky, in the shapeless folds of a drab priest's robe that was held about his middle by a cord. He was Mexican, with a Mexican's ageless dark skin and the black and smoky eyes of the Indian. The light of the altar candles behind him gleamed faintly upon his tonsured skull. His look, though mild, held a faint reproach as it touched the intruder and the gun barrel gleaming in Kincaid's big hand.

He said, patiently, in English, "Yes? I am Father Gregorio. What is it you want of me?"

Kincaid shrugged, scowling. "Nothin', I guess. Some bushwhacker just tried to put a bullet in me. I was lookin' for him."

"You will not find him here."

But, not answering, Kincaid shouldered past and strode inside the mission, still carrying the gun. The church was a long, bare building of mere whitewashed mud, with great, hand-hewn beams, age darkened, crossing the shadowed ceiling. Kincaid came slowly around on his heel, full circle, his narrow glance prowling the room, whose rough walls were hung with Indian blankets and crude holy carvings. There were no pews, and never had been; the gleam of the candles on the poor altar, below the crucifix, put deep shadows into the corners.

Slowly, Kincaid let the heavy six-gun lower to his side at arm's length. And, hearing the whisper of rope-soled sandals on hard-packed earth flooring, he turned again to face the padre.

Father Gregorio's mild features held that same expression of quiet reproach. "I told you," he reminded the other, "that you would not find him in this house." He added, "I heard the shot, myself. It sounded very near—but I think whoever fired it must have made his escape by this time."

"Yeah, I figure the same." Kincaid stuffed the gun away in its holster. And then something—the presence of the holy man, perhaps, or the very atmosphere of that old, candle-lighted mission—caused him belatedly to lift a hand and drag off the sweat-marked Stetson.

"I guess I should apologize," he muttered heavily. "I didn't mean to doubt your word, Padre. I thought there was a chance the guy could have sneaked in here without your knowing it, but"—he looked again about the nearly barren room that held only the whispering silence of the years—"it doesn't seem likely, at that."

"And supposing you had found him?"

Kincaid's answer was harsh, uncompromising. "That would have been between him and me!"

A shadow crossed the other's dark face, but the shoulders under the drab robe merely lifted a little, and Father Gregorio made no answer. And replacing his hat, Kincaid turned and walked directly to the door by which he had entered.

There, however, with a hand on the latch, he hesitated. He looked back, stirred to an unexplained anger. "You disagree?"

"I said nothing."

Kincaid persisted: "But you don't think much of my attitude!"

Pressed for an answer, Gregorio said simply, "It is displeasing to God."

"That's about what I expected to hear you say!" Kincaid touched the grips of his holstered six-gun. "Well, then it's between God and me—and the gent that tried to shoot me out of the shadows. We'll see which the Lord favors, if it comes to a showdown. Me, I can't think He ever really wanted a man to turn the other cheek—or give an enemy a second shot at his back!" He added harshly, "And for that matter, I don't know of any prayer that can turn the force of a bullet!"

The Mexican shook his tonsured head, eyes troubled but without rancor. "You want me to argue your blasphemy," he said. "But as you say, that must be between yourself and

God. I only wonder—are you really as sure in your cynicism as you think? For why, then, are you so quick to make a quarrel?"

Kincaid's glance narrowed. A retort formed in his mind, but he left it unspoken, merely looking at this gentle man through one long and silent minute. Then, abruptly, he swung the door open and stepped again into the darkness, frowning as the ancient wooden panel closed behind him.

He thought, angry with himself: That ambush try has got me more upset than I figured, to make me fly off the handle with a harmless Mex priest!

He felt a quick shame for this, and with it a respect for the calm, quiet-mannered Gregorio. Kincaid was one who admired self-possession; and he had found it here even though rooted deep in a faith which he did not share. To lose his own control in the face of such assurance was a thing that touched him with chagrin.

But it did not matter, really, and he shoved the incident from him and brought his thoughts back to what was, after all, the important thing: Whoever had tried that shot at him was clearly gone. Had he meant murder but lacked the nerve to follow with a second bullet? Or had his aim been only to put a scare into the victim?

Kincaid pondered these questions, standing with the wall of the old mission at his back and the soft darkness about him. And finding no ready answer, he shrugged and turned once more toward the plaza.

Not many minutes had passed, but they seemed enough for this town to have already forgotten its quick flurry of excitement. The square had emptied again; and as Kincaid strode across its dry, baked dust, the crunch of his boots sounded loud to him—night here was that silent, that unstirring.

Someone stood in a waiting attitude under the mesquite-pole roof fronting the big hotel. By the weak flare of a wall lantern next the lobby entrance, Kincaid quickly saw that it was the woman named Irene. He walked directly toward her across the angle of the square.

He was only a few yards away when, with a spinning of

wheels, a buggy came whipping out of the shadows, bearing straight toward him.

The thought struck home that the driver's purpose was to run him down, and he drew back cursing; the bay mare between the shafts missed him so narrowly that its shoulder all but brushed against him and its hoofs spattered him with dust. Then the man on the buggy seat was hauling the reins, bringing his rig to a halt squarely between Kincaid and the woman under the arcade roof.

He felt no surprise to see that the man was Britt Larkin. Their glances met, and even in that poor light Kincaid could read the malevolence looking at him out of the other's hard stare. Afterward Larkin turned to the woman and he said sharply, "Come, Irene! Get in!"

Deliberately, Kincaid walked around the buggy, which had been placed to block him, and moved to the woman's side. She turned as he halted, one hand raised to the brim of his wide hat. He said, "I'm afraid I handled you pretty rough a minute ago. I didn't aim to. I was scared that crazy fool would throw off another bullet and you'd be in the way of it."

She looked into his eyes, frankly regarding him. "I know," she answered finally; and her voice was cool and throaty, well matching her ripe good looks. "It's all right." She smiled—only a brief movement of her lips.

Kincaid sensed the dark disapproval of the man waiting on the buggy seat, heard him shift his position. Giving no heed to this, he pursued the conversation pleasantly: "I won't forget that you came running to help when you saw me hit the ground like I'd been shot. That was mighty kind—toward a stranger in a strange town. I just wanted to thank you."

"Please don't," she said in that melodious voice. "I behaved very foolishly, Mr. Kincaid."

"You know who I am, do you?"

"Oh yes." Her smile took on a deeper, secret amusement as she added: "My husband told me."

Britt Larkin said sharply, "For the last time, Irene! I'm not going to wait all night!"

The threat struck Kincaid as particularly ludicrous, coming from one whose jealousy was much too plain to suppose he would actually let this woman out of his sight. But she did not argue or appear to take offense. She remained where she was an instant longer—just long enough to assert her independence of his will. The smile returned, lingered for a moment on her handsome, spoiled mouth.

Then she turned and stepped into the rig.

Her husband made no move to help her, hunched there bearlike with the reins in his hands and elbows on knees; there was nothing at all gallant or polished in Britt Larkin. But Kincaid had moved quickly to place a hand beneath the woman's elbow and lift her up the iron step of the rig. As she settled into her place, she made a nod of thanks.

At once Larkin had slapped leather against the mare's rump, and they rolled away from the man before the hotel. Irene's face showed palely, still turned toward him, for the instant before the night swallowed up the handsome black rig and its wheels went spinning to silence.

And Ross Kincaid looked after them until the last sound of the buggy was stilled. . . .

Somewhere a guitar's silver tones hung trembling in the early darkness, and a husky voice added the warm and liquid notes of a Spanish love song. A breeze stirred the plaza dust, carrying a parched scent and reminding him of the miles he'd ridden, of the tiredness in all his muscles. But there was yet one detail he must see to before taking the saddle again for the last leg of his day's long riding.

He turned to the bar entrance behind him; but a quick glance showed him that dismal room was empty except for the bartender. As he hesitated, wondering where next to look, a quartet of hands from one of the ranches came loping into town. They tied at a hitch rack across the plaza and trooped inside a whiskey mill, trailing spur sound and whooping, pointless laughter. Such night life as Apache could boast in the middle of a week was beginning. Casually Kincaid walked over there, took a look inside this second saloon; but again with no success.

He made the circuit of the plaza, an operation that did

not take long. Afterward, strongly suspecting that his hunch was a good one, he turned in the direction of the livery stable, where the grulla mare awaited him.

And there, under the barn lantern swaying above the door, he again confronted the gross figure of the sheriff.

The mastiff eyes regarded him foggily; the jowls stirred, and again rumbling speech took shape somewhere deep within the man. "I hear you had trouble with a bush-whacker."

"That's right, Sheriff," murmured Kincaid. "And you're on the job already? It couldn't have happened more than half an hour ago. News certainly travels fast in these little towns!"

His sarcasm was not lost on the official; the sheriff's heavy mouth dragged down into harder lines. He said, "Such talk ain't called for, mister. You think so high of yourself and so damned little of the law, I figure there's no point lettin' you tell me to pull my nose out of your affairs. If some personal enemy has trailed you all the way down here to try his luck, I figure that's your concern."

"Well, and you're right," Kincaid agreed, shortly. "Only it was nobody from outside."

"You're layin' this to one of our local boys, are you?" The lawman's tone was scoffing. "Next you'll be tryin' to make a bushwhacker out of Britt Larkin, I suppose, or Charlie Mayes?"

Coldly the other replied, "I wouldn't waste my breath. Not on ears stopped up with prejudice!"

Kincaid left him standing there and walked up the ramp and into the stable with its warm, horsy smells and rustlings of sound on straw-littered boards.

He found his grulla fed and rested enough for some final trailing, and proceeded to spread the still-wet blanket in place and then pile on the rest of his gear. As he led the horse out of its stall a Mexican hostler came sidling up to him, having kept carefully out of the way until the work was done and it was time to settle the bill. Kincaid paid money into his grubby palm and then asked casually, indicating the rumps and switching tails in the stalls:

"Which bronc belongs to Charlie Mayes?"

The hostler looked at him squarely. "I do not think I have hear this name, señor."

Kincaid handed him a couple more silver dollars. "Now do you remember?"

The cartwheels disappeared into manure-spattered clothing. "A sorrel with a roached mane and one white stocking. Only it is gone. Señor Mayes has left town, quick, maybe a half—three quarters of an hour ago."

"I figured something like that."

Mounting, Ross Kincaid rode out into the plaza.

The sheriff was not in sight; no one appeared to notice the stranger's leaving as he found the south trail and pulled away into the night darkness. A mechanical piano was jangling in one of the saloons, and this monotonous sound followed him a little distance as the last buildings dropped behind.

Then the sound and the shape of the town was lost, and the old mission pointing its cross toward the sky; the changing pattern of black earth and the changeless stars overhead were his only companions.

III   AT BLOCK S

So she was Mrs. Britt Larkin.

This merely added one more to the long, long list of facts a man accepted without necessarily pretending to understand them. Astonishing enough to find a woman like Irene Larkin in a place like this, remote from the refinements of the big towns that must have produced her. To find her actually mated to an unmannered boor like the surly Leaning 7 boss was stretching the limits of belief.

Still, Kincaid had his hard-won knowledge of men and motives and the basic cynicism which the little padre had discovered in him. By his reckoning there could be one, and only one, adhesive factor to bring together the most diverse types of human beings and hold them in a union as unlikely as this marriage was: Money.

And she'd be a pretty expensixe luxury for a gent like
Larkin to hold onto—especially in such forsaken country,
he decided. This Leaning 7 must be a bigger spread than I'd
give it credit for, just looking at him.

Now, however, his conjectures came circling back to another puzzle—a bullet from the shadows, bearing his name
but for the narrow margin of poor light and a hasty aim.
He thought by this time he knew who'd fired that shot
. . . as surely as if he had actually caught a look behind the
gun and seen the sly, narrow face, foxlike with its sharp
eyes and rusty hair. That would be exactly Charlie Mayes'
speed—sneaking behind darkened buildings, waiting for
an enemy to step into his sights. And Charlie would run,
leaving town as quick as he could reach his horse, when he
knew the first try missed.

But what about Britt Larkin—carefully hanging back so
as to let the stranger emerge from the hotel entrance alone,
and calling his wife's name in a frenzy of terror when she
started after Kincaid? To Kincaid it added up just one
way: The ambush had been planned together, between
Larkin and Charlie Mayes. They must have buried their
own personal grudge in the urgent need of destroying this
weapon before it could reach the hands of their mutual
enemy, Ward Sullivan.

Well, in the couple hours since he hit this country he'd
already learned enough to indicate it was a complicated
and dangerous job that awaited him here . . . not, of course,
that he ever expected to be called in for any other kind.
Kincaid's price was a high one, and no man, except in
desperate straits, was apt to think of sending for him. . . .

He rode south and west toward the hills, following the
bartender's brief instructions. This wagon trail took him
a looping course through nearly level country, whose features were only dimly discernible under the high stars. Remembering that one attempt had been made on his life
already and that a second was wholly possible, Kincaid rode
with a strict attention for the shadows. He did not really expect such trouble, though.

He did not believe Charlie Mayes had it in him to ven-

ture another try, once having given his victim warning by
missing the first one.

There were the normal sounds of night, and of the grulla's
slow, rolling gait, beating back from the earth's sounding
board. Once or twice he glimpsed the dark shapes of cattle,
grazing as they drifted. Presently the voice of running water
spoke somewhere ahead.

He approached the fording of a shallow stream that ran
due northward across gravel and between low banks lined
with scrub cottonwood and brush. Here, if anywhere, was
a likely place for ambush, and he came to it with caution,
but found nothing. And just beyond the crossing the trail
forked.

The flickering light of a match showed Kincaid the let-
tering on a three-paneled signpost set where the ways di-
vided. According to this, Block S lay directly ahead along
the middle fork. South, the sign pointed toward Britt Larkin's Leaning 7. On the right was the trail to Star; "C.
Mayes, Owner," he read below the brand.

Kincaid shook out the match and sat for some moments
looking at that split in the trail and hearing the busy murmur of the pebbled stream at the fording he had crossed.
So, it's Sullivan in the middle, he mused aloud, with our
good friends, Mayes and Larkin, squeezing him from either
side. . . . The signpost had told him much, summing up a
situation and a pattern he could understand, having seen
its like a good number of times before. Many a confused
picture of range trouble, he had found, eventually boiled
itself down to something like this.

Frowning thoughtfully, he nudged the grulla and sent it
ahead into the middle fork.

The country became rougher as he drew nearer the curtain of black hills drawn across the western sky. Block S
must be hill graze, though none of the ridges loomed very
big; and if there was water on them, they probably grassed
over well enough.

Somewhere southward of this crumpled region of steep
draws and spiny lumps, mesquite-thickened, would lie the
invisible boundary line of the Mexican border. How many

miles, he was not sure, but he judged it to be no great distance.

The Sullivan ranch buildings, when he came upon them,
sat atop a dry bench under the first lift of the hills. The
trail climbed through a shallow, brush-choked draw. Kincaid watched the lights as he approached, sizing the place
up—a modest enough spread of only a few stone-and-adobe
structures and no elaborate layout of corral pens. A wind-
mill made a clacking sound, its blades turning over slowly
in the still night.

Not a shoestring ranch, maybe, but on the other hand
not a wealthy one. Not one that would normally be importing high-priced guns like Ross Kincaid's. . . .

Now, as the grulla carried him in toward the low-roofed
main house, a feist dog all at once came streaking from
somewhere, snapping and snarling. It whipped back and
forth, pivoting in a half circle about the horse's front feet
and bringing the night alive with its clamor.

The grulla halted uneasily.

Kincaid, annoyed, freed one boot from stirrup and
once, as the dog came too close for wisdom, he caught it
neatly with his toe, gave a swing that sent it looping for a
couple of yards through the air. The cur hit sprawling and
came up with all four legs pumping vigorously before it
could gain traction in the slick grass and leap to renew the
attack, its frenzied howls redoubled.

By this time Kincaid was already moving ahead; he came
toward the house, with the excited dog leaping and snarling about him, and found a man standing in darkness at
the corner of the building.

"Hold where you are!" ordered a voice sharply.

The timbre of the voice gave it away; it was very young
—not yet safe from breaking in moments of excitement,
and the owner of the voice was excited now. Kincaid
thought he saw window light glimmer faintly on the metal
of a gun, and he knew it could be dangerous to ride in on a
weapon in the hands of such a youngster.

But in spite of the command and of the dog that was still
yelping and snarling at his heels, he went straight forward.

And the voice said again, rising a notch and louder now, "Stand hitched, I tell you!"

This time Kincaid halted, frowning narrowly at the gunman whom he could see faintly—a thin-looking shape with a short-barreled carbine leveled in his hands, butt set against one hip. The face, in the glimmer of light from the window, had a bony cast to it under a wild shock of unruly hair. Kincaid sat saddle a moment, motionless, not speaking, while he considered the other.

Now a woman had appeared, silhouetted plainly in the doorway. She spoke sharply above the racket of the yelping dog: "What is it? Who are you?"

"First call off your pup" said Kincaid, and added sourly: "Both of them!"

A few sharp words to the dog finally settled it and brought it whimpering to heel. "And you, Rooster," the woman told the rifle bearer, "put that gun away, will you!"

Rooster lowered the weapon reluctantly, arguing. "I never seen this guy before. What's he doin' at Block S?"

"I'm looking for Ward Sullivan," the stranger answered him.

"Right here," said a second man who at that instant had stepped past the woman and through the doorway. "Do I know you?"

"You sent for me. I'm Kincaid."

The pronouncement of this name caused its quick effect. A gusty breath broke from the one with the carbine that sagged forgotten now in his hands. And Ward Sullivan himself exclaimed, "Of course! We didn't know when we could expect you, or if you would show up at all. . . . But come inside, friend. Rooster, take care of his horse."

At once the lad stepped forward to take the reins Kincaid handed down to him; his wide eyes shone in reflected lamplight from the doorway. But the visitor told him, "Leave the saddle on—until we find out for sure if I'm staying."

Sullivan had drawn aside, inviting him to enter first. Kincaid hesitated, looking at the woman, but she made no move; so he took off his hat, ducking the low lintel as he walked into the house.

It was small enough. Except that a pair of doors led to what he assumed were sleeping quarters, most of it comprised a single room. The furnishings were not elaborate. A wood stove and a trestle table, oilcloth covered, took up much of the space; there was a lamp burning on the table, and the stove would serve both for cooking and, whenever it would be necessary in this climate, for heat.

At the other end of the room an attempt had been made to create a homelike atmosphere by placing two heavy, leather-slung armchairs there with a small table, with a second lamp and a hand-embroidered scarf between them. There was a multicolored rag rug on the bare floor boards in this corner, and the window had been hung with green-and-yellow drapes of some cheap material. Such was the Block S ranch house.

Kincaid's host indicated one of the easy chairs, then quickly amended the invitation, saying, "But likely you're hungry. Some coffee, anyway. There's still some in the pot, I reckon, Claire." He added, "My daughter."

Kincaid threw her a quick look. The light showed her as a young woman of good enough features, but with a certain drab sullenness that clouded her eyes and embittered the shape of her mouth. She said nothing now, merely turning in a half-automatic gesture to reach the graniteware coffeepot off the back of the big stove. He stopped her with a word.

"No, I don't want anything; I ate in town. Thanks, anyhow."

She merely shrugged, as though with indifference, and put back the pot. And as Kincaid followed his host across the room the girl got a basket of mending and took a seat at the trestle table, where she fell to work in silence. Kincaid at once forgot her.

The newcomer slacked into a chair, grunting with tiredness. Sullivan, for his part, remained standing, boots spread wide apart on the rag rug, and taking a battered pipe out of his pocket, began filling it from a blackened rawhide pouch, tamping the mixture into the bowl with a blunt thumb. He said again, "I frankly didn't think you would show up, Kincaid—not this far and for a total stranger."

"Why, I'm generally working for strangers," answered Kincaid briefly. "And I have no objections to seeing new country. Your letter happened to catch me on the wing. I'm surprised, a little, that you were able to get in touch with me."

Sullivan waved this question aside as unimportant. "A mutual acquaintance; he knew I needed help and suggested you, and I took the chance."

He lighted the pipe, tossed the match away. Suddenly he was pacing the floor, seemingly propelled by a restlessness that would not allow him to remain still.

An odd figure, Kincaid thought—not tall but solidly strong. Or, rather, he had a strong man's body, but it was as though something had drained the strength out of him, leaving him empty and tired and yet with this driving restlessness.

Whatever it was, it had aged him also, lining his face and streaking what had been a fine, dark mane of hair with great masses of gray and even solid white. All this Kincaid's expert glance read in the man with puzzlement. There must be something he missed—some fact that explained these things and which he ought to have recognized but somehow failed to.

Apparently Sullivan had misread the other's silence. He said quickly, "Of course I know your services don't come cheap. But I'm ready to meet the tariff."

"We can discuss that later," grunted Kincaid. "First, what makes you so sure I can do you any good? I don't take a man's money unless I figure I'm able to give him something in return."

"You'd not have many doubts if you were in my shoes," Sullivan told him bitterly. "If your enemies had you shoved into a crack so narrow you could scarcely lift a finger to help yourself—and with no other man ready to stand for you—I think then you'd pay any amount for someone with the reputation to make your enemies hold back a little and give you a chance to breathe!"

"These enemies," suggested Kincaid. "You're talking about Britt Larkin and Mayes."

The other man showed his quick surprise. "What do you know about them?"

"I stopped awhile in Apache," Kincaid shrugged. "Let's just say that I got a look at them both. Later, the signpost at the crossing told me a few other things. I'd say they want your range—to split between them. Something like that?"

"Block S owns better grass than either of their spreads," Sullivan explained, "and water—which these hill ranches mainly lack. They both knew that when they moved in here and took land on either side of me. But they figured it wouldn't be hard to get rid of anyone with my record . . ."

Record! Suddenly the last piece clicked into its slot— the missing fact about Ward Sullivan that explained him. Somehow he had forgotten, until that moment, how Britt Larkin had called his enemy a jailbird; now, looking with fresh understanding at the man, Kincaid knew that it completed the picture.

Only prison would have drained the vigor from an active man in this way, yet left him with the restless unease of a caged beast. The dry rot of prison had worked deep into Sullivan; still, it had not utterly corrupted or broken him. Even though it might have cost him youth and health, it had also taught him much.

It had tamed something that was wild in Ward Sullivan. And the eyes that looked at Kincaid out of that young-old face held, in their clear depths, a mildness and wisdom that had been hard-learned but well assimilated. Even in anger and bitterness they seemed to Kincaid the kindest and most thoughtful pair of eyes that he had ever looked into—except, possibly, for one other.

Yes, strange as it might seem, there was something of the same quality in both these men—in the saintly mission priest and in this other who had known the horror of steel bars and stone.

Ward Sullivan was continuing in a level tone, shirking nothing of the story he had to tell. "I'm not proud of my past, but I figure I've paid for the mistakes I made. And there were a lot of them. I was pretty wild, even for a kid; I blotted some brands, and then I got in with a tough bunch and we went into the big-scale stuff. When the law broke it up, the judge figured to be lenient with me. I only got twenty years."

"Twenty years!" echoed Kincaid, aghast. "Just for a little brand blotting?"

"I said it was pretty big scale," the other man reminded him. "And they were determined on a cleanup. The ring-leaders got the rope, or life. Because I was just a youngster, they went easy on me. Then, too, I managed to save some time on good behavior.

"It was long enough, though. What made it worse, I had married a girl just before the law took me. Our child was born while I was in the pen. The mother died, but Claire managed to survive somehow. She was nearly grown before I got out of prison; I brought her here, where we weren't known, and started ranching. And we've done pretty well, too, though we naturally had to start small. We built a pretty fair spread. Then one day this pair of gents showed up who knew me, and what I was . . ."

Mayes and Larkin had come into this country, and they had hatched their scheme. They had moved onto the dry hills flanking Block S on either side—land that was less valuable than this, lacking sufficient water in certain seasons. Then they had launched their campaign by disclosing to Sullivan's neighbors the secret of his past and by whis-perings that turned their suspicions insidiously against him. And when dribblings of missing cattle began to dis-appear into the wastes above the border, these suspicions were to take full and clear shape in open distrust.

The pipe wasn't drawing well and, as he talked, Sullivan fished a clasp knife from his pocket, dug into the bowl with it, his eyes on what his hands were doing. Looking at him, Ross Kincaid knew a welling respect; also, a certain humil-ity before the strength of this man. He made his sufferings brief, his story simple. Yet behind his words lay years of heart-rending agony and the gallant effort to begin again— and, now, the threatened loss of all he had built.

"You understand, I hope," Sullivan said gruffly, "I'm only tellin' you this personal history because, if you take the job, you'll have to know just what you're buckin'."

"The job, then," said Kincaid, summing it up, "is not only to hold your enemies back from Block S graze, but at the same time to prove somehow that if cattle are crossing into Mexico, it's none of your doing."

Sullivan snapped the knife blade shut. "Maybe you see why I'm prepared to pay high!"

Turning abruptly to a small desk that stood against the wall, he raised its drop lid, pulled out a drawer. When he returned, there was a sheaf of money in his hand, and he placed this on the table beside Kincaid, full in the spill of lamplight.

Kincaid looked at the money. He looked at the toes of his dusty boots stretched out before him; and then he lifted his head, and across the room his eyes met those of the girl. For an instant only; then she dropped her glance to the material in her hands, and her face was as reserved and distant, as sullenly cold, as ever. Her stitching went on without interruption. In this stillness, prick of needle and hiss of thread whipping through the cloth made the room's only sounds.

The money lying at his elbow stirred faint anger in Kincaid. There was goodness to this man, but plainly little tact. He should have known that no one likes to have his purchase price plopped down that way—openly, like a stud bull on the block. But Kincaid shrugged his irritation aside, and not yet touching the bills, he asked one other question.

"What would be your idea of proceeding?"

"I'd make you foreman," Sullivan said promptly. "I'd give you a free hand, with the title and reason for being here."

"What about a crew? How are you fixed?"

"Not well. All this talk has scared away the honest riders, and I don't dare risk any other kind. At present I'm down to three men in the bunkhouse."

"Including that kid?"

Sullivan nodded. "Including him. Rooster is a hothead but loyal to his first brand, but he's hardly man-size. Then there's Macready—old Mac—who works for me because no other outfit would be apt to give him anything at his age. And George—I never been able to figure what to make of him. A good enough hand, but he never says nothin' at all. Why he sticks I don't know; sometimes I think he might be a border jumper himself, hanging on here because it's a quick hop and a jump to safety."

"Two men and a boy," repeated Kincaid scowling. "It's a cinch we don't have much to work with. . . ."

"You said, 'we'?" Sullivan looked at him quickly.

Kincaid shrugged. "Why not?"

He lifted out of the chair and, taking the money, folded it and stuffed it into a pocket of his shirt, buttoning it there. "A month's wages. We'll give it that much of a try. If I can't show you any results by then, you don't owe me anything more."

"We could win or lose this fight inside a month," said Sullivan bleakly. "Britt Larkin has already moved in on Dragoon Meadow, knowing I don't have crew enough left to put him off. That fat tub of a sheriff, Port Griswold, won't do anything—naturally. It's up to us."

"Then we'll look into Dragoon Meadow first off. We've got one strong card, and only one," Kincaid went on. "Larkin and Mayes are so sure Block S is through that they've already started fighting over the spoils. I even had them bidding against each other for me in town this evening before they found out I meant to sign with you!"

For the first time Ward Sullivan's tired face lightened. "I wish I could have seen it! I do, indeed!"

And Ross Kincaid decided to leave him with this small ray of hope, though he knew himself it was a dim one. At the first sign of a fight from their beaten enemy, those two would be closing ranks again; they had, in fact, already done so with their try at Kincaid's life. They could sink their differences as long as it was to their advantage. Still, the differences were there; and a clever man must play on them for whatever it could gain him.

Now he saw that Sullivan was offering his hand in a clasp to clinch the deal that they had made. He seemed already to stand a little taller, a little straighter, in his renewed hopes brought by Kincaid's coming.

Their hands met, fell apart. Sullivan said:

"Maybe now we can take the saddle off your horse. And I'll introduce you to the crew."

"Not necessary," Kincaid told him. "I'd rather introduce myself. . . ."

IV   DRAGOON MEADOW

Kincaid slept long and hard, his strong body renewing itself in a single night from the deep tiredness that lay like lead in his veins. The sun was well up when he woke, finally, on the bunk he had taken for himself in the crew's littered quarters. He lay as he was for a few minutes, to enjoy the luxury of blankets and a mattress under him; then he levered himself off the bed and dressed quickly.

Breakfast was ended already for everyone else on the ranch, but at the house Claire Sullivan fried him up a platter of eggs and bacon and poured him a china cup full of black, strong coffee. As he ate, Kincaid watched the girl's movements, cleaning dishes off the oilcloth-covered trestle table, starting them soaking in the sink. Apparently she did all the cooking for the family and the small crew. Her movements were efficient, without waste; but she did everything with a set, sullen look.

When Kincaid asked for a refill of his coffeecup she complied without looking at him; and, observing her work-reddened hands, the shapeless cotton dress that concealed what might have been a rather decent figure, the brown hair that she wore pulled tight in a knot behind her head, he thought: You don't know it, but you're an old maid already!

Still, with her mother dead and her father in prison, she must have grown up knowing nothing but work and hardship. Coldness and hostility toward everything and everybody were likely an ingrained part of her nature by now. He supposed one really had no right to feel anything toward her but a kind of pity, and should forgive her surliness.

He asked for her father; she said shortly, "Out in the barn, I guess," and that was every word she spoke.

When he rose from the table, finally, he thanked her for the grub, but she was rattling dishes in the pan and gave no sign of hearing. He got his hat and went out into the warm sunlight that filled the morning.

It would be hot later; already the sky was taking on the look of heat—especially eastward, where the bench dipped to distant lower land and the blue edge of the heavens whitened as it curved down to meet the earth. The three Block S hands were lined along a bench against the wall of the bunkhouse, the ranch dog curled at their feet. They were obviously waiting for orders from their new foreman. He walked over that way.

He had spared little time for these men last night after the first brief introductions in the bunkroom. Now he gave them each a more careful sizing up.

It struck him that Sullivan had described them well. The old fellow they called "Mac" was a dried-up little ancient, with a face that looked crumpled together and watery blue eyes whose lids had a narrow line of red all round their inner edges. Just now his knotted, arthritic hands were trying to show Rooster how to shape a quirly, and the youngster, with paper and tobacco, was striving without success to imitate Macready's movements.

It seemed to be an often repeated lesson; when the boy's fingers fumbled their work and the wheat paper broke and spilled tobacco down across his plaid shirt and jeans, old Mac vented a cackle of disgust. "I swear, it don't 'pear likely I could teach nothin' to anythin' as clumsy as you!"

The kid flushed deeply, slapping the shred tobacco from his clothing. "Aw hell!" he grunted. "Gimme another try, Mac! Just one!"

"Nope! Nope!"

Macready lifted an elbow to ward off his grab, at the same time pulling the drawstring of the tobacco sack with his teeth and stuffing it and his book of papers into a vest pocket. "I'm about through lettin' you waste my makin's for me!"

Deftly he twisted the tube into shape, hung it in the corner of his mouth. "You never learn to build 'em, you'll never get the habit of smokin' 'em," he pointed out as he fished up a match and cracked it alight on his horny thumbnail. "Be the better for it."

Then talk broke short as Ross Kincaid came and halted before the bench.

Smoking forgotten, young Rooster instantly jerked up straight, the big eyes in his bony, red-burned face fastened on his new boss. The respect he held for the legend of Ross Kincaid had been only too apparent from the instant he had first learned the newcomer's identity. Kincaid avoided the boy's too intent stare, looked at the third man —the silent one who seemed to be known only by the name of George.

There was a person, he thought, who would need some watching. He had the look of a common working hand, but these secretive men naturally roused doubts; and though George seemed to show no hesitancy in meeting a questioner's eyes directly, Kincaid had so far heard little from him more demonstrative than a grunt.

Kincaid saw no reason for equivocation as to his own presence here. He said now, "You all know who I am. Whether Sullivan has told you his plans or not, you probably have figured out for yourselves what my being on the payroll is likely going to mean."

"Sure," agreed Rooster quickly. "A scrap."

"That's about right. And it may start soon, and it may be a tough one, because I've only got a month. . . . If anybody feels that that's not what he signed on for, maybe we better have an understanding about it right now. Nothing will be said if you want to quit."

He looked flatly from one to the other of the trio on the bench. It was old Mac who answered, shifting his body to a more comfortable position and crossing his withered legs. "If we was afraid of fightin' for our brand," he pointed out dryly, "there's been plenty of chances to get out before now, and don't think we wouldn't!"

"That's damn right!" agreed Rooster. "We ain't run yet, have we?"

"Sullivan," Mac went on, "is a right man—one of the best I ever knew, whatever anybody wants to call him. I don't know as I'm likin' you any better, Kincaid, for suggestin' I'd want to leave him in the lurch!"

A quick glance at the silent George drew no comment, but the very stolidness with which he sat there, idly fondling the silky ears of the ranch hound told him his answer. Kincaid nodded.

"All right," he said. "I didn't mean to make anyone sore; I wanted to be certain we all understood each other. . . . Get horses—and guns," he added crisply. "We're heading for Dragoon Meadow!"

His meaning eluded them for a moment. Then Rooster came off the bench with a shout, his uncertain voice breaking in the middle of it. "Hell! You sure don't figure to waste any time, do you?"

"Why, we've got to start pushing back before they're set for it," said Kincaid. "And then keep pushing. Otherwise they've got the power to run right over us!"

"That sounds like it might make sense," old Mac opined, and unhitched his warped body.

Leaving them, Kincaid walked into the barn and there found Sullivan working with currycomb and brush on a tall, black stallion, sweating over the job but with something of quiet satisfaction in his face. Sullivan rapped his comb against a stall post to knock the hairs from it, pointed with it in pride at the horse.

"Like him?"

Hands in hip pockets, Kincaid walked around the stall to view the black from every angle. He noted the deep barrel, the proud carriage of the head, the long, strong legs set wide apart for speed. But he did not miss, either, the fierce suspicion of the eye that returned his look.

"A handsome animal," Kincaid agreed finally. "But I think there's a devil in him."

Sullivan laughed. "That's his name!"

He laid a hand caressingly on the sleek, black flank; at his touch, a quiver flickered along the muscles beneath the hide of the horse so that the glossiness of it seemed to run like water. One ear lay back as the black swung its head a little, picked up a hoof, and stamped uneasily in the straw.

"Diablo has no master but himself," said Sullivan. "But one of these days, maybe, we'll come to an agreement. One of these days . . ." He gave the flank a friendly slap as he turned away. "There's a kind of truce between us," he went on, swinging the stall door shut. "He likes me to work over him, and sooner or later he'll let me put him under a saddle. He already knows we're friends."

"You haven't tried riding him yet?"

"I've had the bridle and the saddle blanket on; that's the most since I roped him, wild, out of a box canyon in the hills. Some men would have thrown him in the breaking corral long ago. But I want him to be tamed—not broken. That's not right for any horse . . . no more than for a man."

He spoke quietly, but his words held a depth of feeling. And Kincaid understood.

This Ward Sullivan, who had been broken and thrown aside, would redeem his self-respect if he could only win the respect and trust of a free creature like the black. It was a thing he needed, a medicine to restore his spirit. When he could sit upon the back of the stallion and feel it respond willingly, without resentment, to his voice and his hand on the reins, that day would Ward Sullivan be able once more to hold his head high before his fellow men.

"I wish you luck with him," said Kincaid, and he meant it.

He told Sullivan, then, his intentions of taking the crew on a morning jaunt to Dragoon Meadow. The other listened without comment, only nodding a little.

"When I hired you," he said finally, "I gave you a free hand. Dragoon Meadow will be as good a place as any to make a show of strength. It was a plain steal when Larkin sent his men in there to take over my line cabin and put his cattle on my water and grass." He added hesitantly, "Of course, I think you understand I'm hoping the threat of force can win enough so that real force may not be needed."

"I know. But I wouldn't count on it. Maybe," Kincaid suggested, "you'd rather not come along this morning."

"I'm coming," said Sullivan quietly. "We'll leave no doubts in their minds that I'm backing you to the limit. Besides, if old Macready and the kid are willing to ride into a thing like this, on my account, my place is beside them. . . ."

Kincaid found his grulla tied to a corral post, already saddled and waiting for him, his rifle thrust in its place beneath the stirrup fender. He stopped short, looking about in puzzlement, to see young Rooster grinning at him, eager-eyed, from the hull of a piebald gelding. And without knowing exactly why, he felt a kind of irritation.

There had been no heroes in Ross Kincaid's boyhood, and so hero-worship was a quality for which he held small respect. It gave him a feeling of physical uneasiness to have his every movement and every smallest item of his belongings made an object of intent and careful observation.

He noticed how the saddle blanket had been smoothed, just so; how the lass rope had been recoiled and fastened carefully to the horn string. He offered Rooster a curt nod, which the lad could interpret, if he liked, as thanks for his trouble; but he also made a point of checking the cinches, giving them a jerk to show that he was not entirely satisfied with the way the job had been done.

Then he lifted into leather. "Let's ride!"

A figure in the shadow of the ranch-house doorway watched, unmoving, as they went streaming out of the ranch yard. He could still see her standing there when he looked back for the last time, just before a hill shoulder rose to block his view of the buildings. . . .

They went, the five of them, across hills of brown grass and mesquite, pushing south and east under a burning sky—Sullivan, at Kincaid's stirrup, pointing out landmarks, with the three crewmen bunched behind them. The range looked good enough for being hill graze, and the cattle they sighted wearing the Block S iron tallied well to Kincaid's critical eye. Sullivan had got off to a late start, perhaps, and he had not had his choice of land. But what he had managed to build here was well worth a fight to hold onto.

Toward noon they halted atop a ridge grown over with stunted cedar and pine, and saw Dragoon Meadow ahead

of them—tawny yellow, with the glint of water. Cattle were
scattered across the meadow, feeding. At the foot of this
low ridge, the mud-and-shake line cabin stood, and a small
mesquite-pole corral had a couple of horses running in it.
A blue line of smoke curled upward from the iron stovepipe
chimney.

"Well, there it lies," Sullivan grunted. "That's Larkin
beef you see—brought in through the gap yonder." He
pointed out a low pass between two hill spurs that flanked
the meadow some three hundred yards south of where they
sat. "He's been keeping a pair or more of his tough hands
in that shack ever since, with nothing to do but oil their
guns and wait for us to make any move. Hasn't seemed
worth the losses it would cost us trying to take it back."

Kincaid rubbed the flat of a thumb along his gaunt jaw,
considering the setup. It appeared quiet enough—almost
too quiet. Somehow, he had not quite believed that Larkin would fail to guess what his first move would be and
to take measures against it.

"All right," he announced, forming his strategy. "No
use to charge in with guns spitting and let 'em pick us off
through the windows. . . . We haven't shown ourselves
yet. Ward, you take George and try working down through
the timber into those cottonwoods on the shack's blind
side. Mac and I will give you time enough, and then we'll
ride on in and see what reception we get. If you two only
keep out of sight, we should be able to put them into a
pincers. How does that sound?"

"I like it," agreed Macready; and Ward Sullivan nodded
and said, "We'll play it that way."

"But what about me?" Rooster wanted to know.

"You're to stay put and keep a watch from here. I figure
Larkin just might have a surprise planned for us. If you
notice anything funny, fire off a cartridge and give us a
chance to find cover." The youngster was plainly disap-
pointed, but Kincaid gave him no time to protest. "Let's
go!" Kincaid ordered. "Your move first, Sullivan."

The older man looked a little white over the seriousness
of the thing to which he had agreed to commit his men,
but without hesitation he reined away into the thick

growth crowning the slope, and the silent George fell in behind him. Watching anxiously until they had gone from sight, Kincaid decided there was little likelihood of anyone in the shack below detecting their movements. He made a slow count, not crowding the other pair. When he thought they had waited long enough he spoke to Macready and sent his grulla boldly forward.

They dropped down the ridge, unhurriedly, through the sweet scent of cedars, loose soil sponging up their hoof sound and tree shadows sliding in bands across them. Presently this scattered timber fell away and, the land leveling off, they were moving across the meadow's cured grass, following a trail directly toward the line shack. And still there was no sign of alarm. Nothing stirred except for the cattle feeding yonder near the spring, the twisting lift of smoke from stovepipe chimney.

When they were still some fifty yards from the shack, its door opened and a man stepped outside.

He was in his undershirt and carried a pan of slops. A flour-sack apron was tied above his jeans. He emptied the pan in a flash and slap of dirty water against the earth; then, seemingly, he caught his first sight of the two riders approaching. Tossing the pan onto a bench beside the open doorway, he stood motionless, one bone-thin arm lifted to shield his eyes as he watched them cover the remaining distance.

There was a six-gun shoved into his waistband behind the apron, but he made no move to touch it . . . though it occurred to Kincaid, suddenly, that a man does not normally wear a gun in his belt when he is at work cooking or cleaning up afterward. Something in this thought struck a jarring note.

Before the shack, now, Kincaid checked the grulla, and Macready pulled in, a little to one side. The man stayed where he was, sullen eyes moving shiftily and not quite focusing on either of the newcomers.

Kincaid said gruffly, "What's this one's name?"

"They call him Dunc," Macready answered. "Watch him—he's tricky."

"I'm watching!"

The scrawny throat bulged as the man swallowed. "What do you want?" he demanded hoarsely. "Takin' up a man's time when he's busy . . ."

"You're going to be a sight busier in a couple minutes. You're going to start moving cattle."

"The hell you say!" cried Dunc. "I don't even know you, mister. I take my orders from Jack Beach, and nobody else!"

"Beach?" echoed Kincaid.

Macready answered. "Larkin's range boss. You'll likely know him when you see him: a big bruiser of a hellion, and a pretty fast gun . . ."

Kincaid was hardly listening, his attention narrowed on the Leaning 7 man. Dunc's shifty eyes were busy again, moving past the riders and searching out the ridge over which they'd come. And all at once the uneasy, nagging wariness at the back of Kincaid's thoughts spoke a sharp compelling warning: He's looking for the others! He knows there were more than two of us, and he's trying to worry out what became of the rest!

Concealing the thrill of alarm this sent through him, Ross Kincaid lifted his head and ran a slow and studied glance across the dark windows of the shack, the meadow, and the rimming hills beyond. His look touched upon the gap which, Sullivan had told him, funneled through the hills toward Leaning 7. Was it mere suspicion, or did he really detect hidden movement in the brush that cloaked its mouth?

All at once the inner voice was shouting: You're in a trap! This guy was the bait, and you rose to it!

V   BULLETS IN THE SUN

A hard ridge of muscle bunched dangerously along his gaunted jowls, but that was his sole outward reaction. Very deliberately he turned and tossed his split reins over into Mac's gnarled hands, saying, "Take 'em, Mac." And then, unhurrying, he lifted a leg across the cantle and dropped to the ground, facing the man called Dunc. There was nothing to indicate what he meant to do.

Dunc wet his lips with a nervous tongue and faded back half a step, allowing one bony hand to inch up across the flour-sack apron toward the jutting gun handle. But then his stare suddenly jerked past Kincaid; at the same instant the latter caught a pad of cantering hoofs coming from the direction of the ridge trail.

Risking a glance, he saw in chagrin the rider was Rooster Adams. He cursed silently. But it was too late now to yell the youngster back. Kincaid moved straight ahead, not pausing in the play that he had started.

A single stride carried him against the man in the doorway. Dunc, breaking, grabbed wildly for his gun; but by then Kincaid was already on top of him, and a hard slash of a wrist knocked his hand away. At the same moment Kincaid had lifted his own six-shooter out of leather while his continuing stride forced the cook backward, crowding him in across the threshold.

Terror choked a cry from the man. After that they both were inside . . . and a hurried scramble of boot leather sounded over near a window at one corner of the room. Kincaid glimpsed a moving shape, the quick spurt of flame as a gun's report shook the flimsy building. He felt Dunc jerk sharply in his grasp, then go limp and sag against him. Pushing him away, Kincaid had his own gun leveled now, and he touched the trigger twice, his second shot mingling with another stab of muzzle flame from that other weapon.

With a hoarse shout of pain, the man at the window stumbled sideways, struck the edge of the sash, and clawed his way down to lie in a huddle below it. There was plainly no one else within the small, single room of the cabin. Kincaid gave only a glance to the lifeless Dunc, knowing the cook had been killed by that first hasty shot. Stepping over him, he moved through powder stink to examine the other man briefly. This one was alive, the shock of lead through a shoulder not yet worn off.

Kincaid gave the fellow's smoking gun a kick and sent

it spinning across the floor, then turned to spear a look through the window.

Outside Macready had freed a belt gun and was just in the act of swinging down from saddle. Kincaid yelled at him, "Quick! Grab that fool Rooster, Mac, and get the horses out of firing range. Look what's heading our way!"

One leg lifted, Macready swiveled about and saw what Kincaid meant. There were five of them—a knot of horsemen spilling from the mouth of that gap yonder, where they had hidden until the break of shooting at the cabin had foced them out. Macready, cursing, dropped into leather again and gave his mount's reins a yank that pulled it savagely about, starting it for the safety of the shack's corner, with Kincaid's grulla trailing.

Shifting for a better look at the oncoming riders, Kincaid's foot knocked something clattering, and he saw it was a saddle gun that had been leaning against the wall beneath the window. Quickly he sheathed his revolver and picked up this weapon, jacking open the breach to see the shine of a copper cartridge under the firing pin. He went to one knee then, the Winchester at high port, staring through the window as he waited for the approaching riders to come within reach of a .30-.30 shell.

They were nearing fast, dust spurting under shod hoofs, sunlight touching glints from harness metal and from the guns they carried. Kincaid noted the bulk of their leader, marking him as the range boss, Jack Beach; and he quickly divined the nature of this trap that had been prepared here.

It had been altogether wise to hold Britt Larkin in wary esteem: Larkin had guessd last night that the coming of Kincaid would mean danger first at Dragoon Meadow, and he had lost no time in sending reinforcements. Their lookout, spotting the approach of Sullivan's crew, had given Jack Beach time enough to lay his trap. Only Kincaid's own canniness in splitting up his men had kept its jaws from closing.

Now, the pair at the cabin already knocked out of the fight, Kincaid waited, with borrowed rifle ready. Slowly he brought it to his shoulder, set the point of his left elbow against the window sill to steady his aim as he narrowed on a bead. His target, naturally, was the big shape of the leader. He held fire until he knew the range was good, and squeezed trigger.

The stock slammed his shoulder. Black powder smoke, quickly filming, hid the field, but as it lifted he saw that the rifle must have shot low. For Jack Beach's horse was down, thrashing in the browned grass. The other riders had scattered apart with startled yells, breaking the easy bunching that made his first shot a sure hit. And still they came on.

He leveled and fired again, missing this time. And then suddenly Ward Sullivan and the rest of the Block S crew were bursting around either end of the cabin to ride out and meet the attack head on.

In a couple of strides Kincaid had made the door, shouting, "Mac!"

Macready heard him, reined aside long enough to toss him down the grulla's leathers; then he was gone in the wake of young Rooster, who stood high and long-legged in the stirrups, whooping like a Comanche and brandishing a six-gun wildly. Sullivan and the older men rode in silence. This was not any wild picnic to them.

Reaching for saddle horn, Kincaid thought better of it and instead dropped the split reins, set a boot to anchor them as he again snapped the rifle to his shoulder. The two bunches of riders had joined now, handguns working on both sides. But he found a target and threw off three shells as fast as he could work trigger and ejector lever. Despite the off-center fire of the unfamiliar weapon, his third shot tallied. A Larkin rider took his bullet and went spinning backward out of saddle.

Larkin's men had checked a little their own rush, meeting this unexpected charge by the Block S crew. Frightened horses were milling confusedly out there on the grass, dust lifting under stamping hoofs to mingle with powder-smoke drift. Kincaid thought it was old Macready who scored the next hit and caused one of the remaining Leaning 7 riders to drop his gun and grab saddle horn as he doubled up, sagging dangerously.

Kincaid swooped up the reins, vaulted into saddle. Only a pair of the enemy was left, and you could almost watch the fight drain out of them. As they moved to pull about and make a run for saftey, Kincaid sang out, "We want those two! Hold them!"

His men, hearing, struck the spurs. In another moment the Leaning 7 men had been surrounded and, at a command, dropped their weapons, waited in sullen silence for their captors to close in.

As quickly as that, the trap laid by Jack Beach for the unsuspecting Sullivan crew had backfired and ended in disaster.

Ross Kincaid cantered up to the knot of stamping horses, Sullivan and his men close-herding the disarmed Larkin riders. He looked the prisoners over briefly, made a careful check to see that none of his own men had been seriously hurt.

The fighting had been too brief and too wild. Macready's saddle had been torn up by a long, gouging slash of a bullet. A trickle of blood showed on George's arm, but he merely shrugged aside Kincaid's question. Rooster Adams was white-faced, trembling with the aftermath of excitement.

"It looks as though we won," Ward Sullivan said.

"Could have been a lot worse," Kincaid agreed briefly. "A wonder that it wasn't. . . . George," he added, tossing over the captured Winchester for him to snatch from the air, "keep this pair covered while we gather in the rest and see how much damage we did. There's a couple in the shack, one dead; fetch the other, Mac. And the one that you shot. I'll take me a look at Jack Beach."

The range boss lay not far from his downed horse that had ceased its thrashing and was already stiffening in death. Pushed halfway to a sitting position, he stared dazedly as Kincaid, with Sullivan and the Rooster in his wake, came loping toward him; then clear thought broke through, and as his head jerked up, the slap of Beach's hand striking holster leather was audible.

The gun, however, had been bounced from its sheath, and he looked wildly about him, quickly found the gleam of the weapon in the grass. Before he could scramble after it, Kincaid's warning came to hold him.

"Let it alone, Jack!" Kincaid had pulled rein, and his own Colt barrel, resting along his thigh, was slanted full at the other man. "Just forget about the gun. On your feet!"

Slowly Beach climbed to a stand, to glare at the horseman through black hair that streamed into his angry face. He had broad, flat cheeks that were blue with a beard that lay just below the skin, where no razor would ever touch it. He was big, all right, his body almost misshapen because of the heavy weight of muscled shoulders above a saddle-whipped wedge of leanness.

He said heavily, "You're Kincaid?"

"Larkin told you, I guess. Was it you, or Larkin, that planned this little shindig? Friend, you should have planned it better. . . ."

A taut muscle flickered under the man's beard-dark cheek like the beat of a pulse. His eyes held pin points of tawny fire. He was dangerous, right enough—even at a moment like this. He said flatly, "This is Britt Larkin's graze. We took it over because Sullivan hadn't crew or cattle enough to hold it."

"Well, and now we've taken it back."

"I wouldn't be too sure!"

Kincaid favored him with a long, impersonal stare, as though weighing his words and not the man himself. "Get his gun and hand it to him, Rooster," he ordered finally. "Empty. . . ."

"Sure, boss!"

The kid was already out of saddle to fish Beach's Colt from the grass and shake the brass out of it, scattering the shells like a handful of bright metal seed. He also picked up the hat Beach had lost and brought it over too, a boyish grin splitting his freckled, bony face. "Your popgun, Mr. Beach," he said, shoving the empty weapon into holster. "And this!" He jammed the hat on Beach's head, shapelessly.

Beach cursed and snatched it off, glaring murderously as he straightened the headgear. Kincaid, watching, saw that the boy was going too far, and he said, "Cut it out, Rooster!"

He decided the youngster must have taken bullying off this man some time in the past and was using the opportunity to get back at him; he lacked enough mature sense to realize he was only storing up trouble for himself, some other day when Kincaid and his gun might not be on hand to equalize the difference. . . .

Right now, the tally was two Leaning 7 men dead and one so blind hurt from a belly wound that he could scarcely cling to his horse's back. The rest, however, were in shape to move cattle; and after a quick doctoring job had been done on the wounded and Jack Beach had angrily stripped his gear off the dead horse and transferred it to one of those in the corral, Kincaid put them to work.

Riding out onto the meadow, they got the grazing cattle roused and turned southward into the gap. There were perhaps a hundred head of Leaning 7 beef, and they purely did not want to be pushed off this grass and away from this water. Even after the main body had been started, recalcitrant steers tried to break free and cut back between the horsemen.

They made it a sweaty job, and Beach and the other prisoners carried their share glumly, taking out some of their angry spite on the cattle and on their horses. Afterward, when the beef was at last moving steadily onto Larkin graze, Jack Beach rode through drifting dust to where Kincaid and Sullivan sat watching the work. His eyes were dark and stormy.

He said, without preface, "It's been a pretty cheap victory. It won't happen this way again."

Kincaid was coiling his lass rope with deliberate movements. He pulled it all in and fastened it to the horn string before he answered. "You're right. Next time—if there is a next—you won't get off so easy."

"Easy?" A sneer darkened Beach's stare as it flicked over Sullivan's ragtag crew. "With this behind you? You talk big!"

Deliberately Kincaid reached, gathered the man's shirt front into a twisting handful, and dragged him nearly out of saddle. "Sure, I talk big," he snapped, his eyes cold daggers, "because I know what I can produce! With this crew behind me, I'm ready to whip Britt Larkin any time he wants me to try! And that's a promise!" He released his hold contemptuously, jerked his head at the swaying figure of the wounded gunman and at the pair of bodies that were tied, arms and legs dangling, across the back of the one spare horse. "Take them along," he snapped, "and just tell Larkin what I told you!"

White with rage, it took Jack Beach a moment to regain control after Kincaid set him free. "Yeah!" he managed finally, his voice husky with restrained fury. "Yeah! You bet—I'll tell him!"

. . . They watched the dust stain of the driven cattle crawl south through the hills onto Leaning 7 grass. They all knew that the recapture of Dragoon Meadow was merely the opening skirmish in this war; but it had been a heartening success, and now that the job was done an excitement of relaxed tension showed through cracks in the grim exteriors of the Sullivan crew.

Ross Kincaid, however, felt small elation. He had done a job, and already he was looking ahead to the next maneuver. Moreover, there was a problem of discipline which, distasteful as it was, he knew could not be put off. He shifted in the saddle, and his tone as he spoke Rooster's name brought him a startled look, the grin fading from the youngster's lips.

"I gave an order a little while ago," he snapped. "I told you to stay on the ridge when we moved down—and you didn't do it. Instead, you let us all ride straight into a trap!

"Maybe you thought I was only talkin'. Or maybe you haven't got it straight, yet, whose orders you take around here! Which, kid?"

Rooster had lost all color, so that the freckles were big, unhealthy blotches against his sickly pallor. He broke gaze now, eyes falling before Kincaid's stare. He looked at his saddle horn and the bony hand clutching it in a grip that stretched the skin tight across the knobby knuckles.

"Well, what about it?" Kincaid repeated, his voice raised a notch. "The next time do you figure to make up your own mind about doing as you're told? At the risk of getting us all murdered?"

He waited. A hard silence had settled on the group. Kincaid heard Ward Sullivan make a sound of distress in his throat, wanting to break in and ease the hardness of this treatment but somehow holding back. He held his own eyes coldly on the bowed head of the boy and waited until he had wrung from him a muffled exclamation of "Sorry!"

"We'll see . . . I'm gonna put you in that Dragoon Meadow camp for the next few days to watch out for a try by Larkin to take it back—and I want you to keep your eyes open. But get this straight: Under no circumstances, if you see trouble shaping, are you to try and fight it alone. You're to tail it straight to headquarters for help. Do you understand?"

"Yessir," said Rooster humbly.

Macready could hold himself in no longer. In spite of Kincaid's dangerous mood, he dared a quick protest. "The kid made a mistake, sure. But that could be a tough assignment you're handin' him, Kincaid! Let me do it."

"No! He signed on to fill a man's job; he's got to learn what it means. If you want," he added, relenting, "you can move your gear out and help hold down the camp at night—two on the job will be better, after dark, until we see for sure what Larkin is going to try next. But I can't spare more than one during workin' hours . . . and he's appointed. You think you can follow orders this time, kid?"

Then Rooster straightened, and his eyes met Kincaid's levelly. "Yessir," he said firmly. "I can." And, jerking reins, he wheeled his pony around and struck the spurs.

Watching him ride away, Kincaid could feel the solid wave of disapproval that beat at him from the circle of silent men; yet he knew that he had done only what was necessary. To survive in a war such as this one promised to be, Rooster would have to grow up fast. And only iron discipline could mature him.

And so there was satisfaction in knowing that the straight look Rooster gave him had held no bitterness, no resentment. It was simply the look of one who has erred, and has taken his punishment, and knows why.

It meant that despite one impetuous error, the youngster had worth-while stuff in him. Rooster would make a hand.

VI   TWO MEN AND A WOMAN

To give Kincaid a better idea of his job, Ward Sullivan showed him over Block S that day, pointing out the condition of the range and of his sparse herds that grazed it. He showed Kincaid the unmarked boundary lines which separated these acres from the adjoining Mayes and Larkin spreads. Pulling up finally on a high, wind-swept spine of granite, they had a long view of all that country, far across the slants and benches to the distant sparkle of Apache Creek and the dun stretching of the lower range. They dismounted to consider this wide vista.

"Desert, west of us," Sullivan explained. "Desert anywhere in this country, for that matter, except where there's water to bring it to life. The really rich graze is down along the creek in the valley. We have the pick of what's left."

"Reason enough for trouble," Kincaid observed. "Reason enough for your enemies to use every crooked trick to try and turn the rest of the range against you. . . . What about this talk of rustling that they've been keeping alive? How much is there behind it?"

For answer, Sullivan indicated the sweep of the high country to south and east. "You see how these hills take a fishhook curve, rounding in the head of Apache Valley where the creek starts? The Mexican border lies only a few miles beyond. And the hills are mostly empty—bare rock and greasewood, full of holes as a sieve. Any dark night it's easy enough to cut out a few head of valley beef and dribble them through. And in time it adds up.

"John Dalhart, Ed O'Malley, Diego Ortiz—those brands have been the big losers . . . at least, they've made the most complaints to the sheriff's office. But Port Griswold isn't built for saddle work, and they should have known as much when they elected him. The cattle thieves slip right through his fingers. Even so, I guess he's run off a good many pounds of lard busting a saddle through that desert country. I honestly think he's tried."

"Larkin and Mayes? They claim to lose much?"

Sullivan lifted his shoulders. "After all, why would rustlers worry about us here when there's all that prime beef down below to whittle at?"

"It's never occurred to anyone, I suppose, that these bench neighbors of yours might be the ones who are doing the whittling."

"Mayes and Larkin," the other pointed out harshly, "don't have prison records!"

Kincaid nodded. "I see what you mean. . . ." He added, "Well, maybe before we're through we'll turn up something to help make folks forget about yours. Maybe we can change the run of their suspicions!"

Ward Sullivan turned his graying head slowly and favored his new foreman with a long, appraising look.

"Somehow," he murmured, "you make me think it can be done! I'm almost ready to believe, after what happened this morning at Dragoon, that we're going to win this fight—that you're to be the salvation of me . . . and my girl."

"I wouldn't bank on it!" Kincaid spoke gruffly, turning back to his waiting horse. "We'll see what a month can do. As for this morning, it could have ended in disaster with that yearling, Rooster, disobeying orders. We played in luck, is all."

"I know," Sullivan agreed soberly. "I thought at first you were pretty hard on the boy—but, maybe not. He's got to learn that a war is no picnic, and every man must take his orders or endanger all the rest. Still, I can't help but worry about what might happen if Larkin makes another move to take the Meadow back again, and nobody but the kid to stop him. . . ."

In leather, Kincaid considered, narrow-eyed. "You've got a point," he agreed. "I should have made myself a little clearer when I laid down the law to Jack Beach. . . ." He took the reins with a sudden purpose. "Well, there's time to remedy that!"

"Where are you heading?" Sullivan demanded.

Across his shoulder he answered, "To pay a call on Britt Larkin!"

He was gone before Sullivan could do more than call futile protest at the risk he would be running.

. . . Leaning 7 headquarters shaped up as a neat group of adobe buildings, placed on a gentle slope with a line of cottonwoods to break the sun's worst glare of afternoon. To frequent whitewashings, a needed touch of color had been added by the setting out, around the house, of all the brightest flowers in the most vivid hues that this country could produce.

Some were desert plants, but others would have to be kept alive at the cost of constant waterings. It was an expensive luxury of beauty—a testimonial to Irene Larkin's vanity and dissatisfaction with all this harsh land.

Kincaid approached warily, but his busy stare found no activity at bunkhouse or corrals or barn, or at the open-fronted blacksmith's shed. He rode under the flickering leaves of the cottonwoods, and halted before the mesquite-pole gallery that shaded the front of the house and made its interior, beyond the gaping door, seem altogether as dark and cool as a cave entrance. While the grulla jingled its bit chains, he twisted slowly in the saddle for a long, final look about him, almost convinced that the place was indeed deserted and that he had wasted the ride here.

Then, movement in the doorway brought him whipping around, starting a quick gesture toward his holstered gun.

His hand checked itself, dropped away from the jutting gun butt; Kincaid eased slowly back into saddle while Irene Larkin, leaning in the doorway with arms folded across her breast, laughed at him throatily.

Her voice was utterly controlled, even though she must know the truth of what she said when she told him, "I'm afraid I nearly got myself shot!"

"Sorry!" grunted Kincaid, for a moment at a disadvantage. "I didn't know what kind of welcome to expect, around here!"

"A bold man!" she murmured, but her voice mocked him.

Looking at her, he wondered frankly why he really had come. Was he a man delivering a warning to an enemy— or only a male seizing on this excuse to do a little tom-catting on another's preserve?

Suddenly his lips quirked, warping into a brash grin; he shoved his sweat headpiece back with a thumb and shifted over to an easier position in the saddle. "Bold enough," he grunted. "I calculate the risks of taking what I want."

The woman returned his stare, coolly. "I'm sure you do."

She was dressed in native fashion, far different from his first glimpse of her last night. She wore a Mexican skirt of strong and vivid color that clung softly to her hips and long thighs, and a wide-necked blouse that bared one shoulder and the cleft in the beginning swell of her bosom. To complement the strong hues of this casually provocative costume, she had artfully heightened the coloring of her cheeks and the contour of her lovely, spoiled mouth . . . and all this, Kincaid thought ironically, wasted on the brutish Britt Larkin and perhaps a dozen sweating ranch hands.

"Your husband, now," he said gruffly. "Not that he's as much to look at, but since my business is with him, perhaps he's the one I'd ought to see."

She shrugged. "I wouldn't know where he is—or when he'll be back. You can wait if you want to. You could probably find something to drink, and it's cooler inside than out here in the sun."

Kincaid's grin broadened, his eyes bold upon her. "Why, sure! Now that I'm here, I see no reason to hurry away again. Yeah, maybe I will wait."

"Suit yourself."

Indifferent, Irene Larkin turned back into the house, the skirt swaying and clinging to her bare calves. He watched until the cool darkness swallowed her, then deliberately swung down and anchored the grulla's reins and followed the woman inside.

Seated at a table in the squalid shack which housed himself and his Star Ranch crew, Charlie Mayes mauled a dog-eared pack of Bicycle cards—not dealing, merely letting the pasteboards slide and blur between his hands as he glowered moodily at nothing. His mouth was still sore and swollen from Kincaid's fist; his thoughts were black ones.

He slammed the deck down on the table suddenly, was just reaching for a whiskey bottle at his elbow when he heard riders approaching across the stillness of afternoon.

He got up kicking back his chair, the bottle in one hand and the cork in the other, and went to the doorway. There were two of them, threading through the chaparral and leaving a stain of lifted dust in their wake. With a horseman's instinct he looked at the mounts, not at the men, and instantly recognized Britt Larkin's gray and the white-stockinged roan that was one of Jack Beach's string.

Guessing at the purpose of this visit, he rammed the cork home and turned to toss the bottle onto a bunk's rumpled blankets. Then, stepping out into sunlight, he waited with hands shoved into hip pockets as the new-comers cantered up to a halt and a ground wind carried away the dust and settled it.

There was no exchange of greetings. Britt Larkin came down at once, his broad face showing displeasure; Beach dismounted more slowly and threw reins like his boss. Yesterday, had this pair from Leaning 7 ridden in on Star in such fashion, Mayes would probably have met them with a hand set carefully on the butt of a holstered six-gun: things had reached that dangerous a state between them. Today, however, all was suddenly changed. The rivalry still remained, but it would wait now in the face of a common danger.

Charlie Mayes jerked his head toward the door, and they followed him in, into a stale mingling of sweat and booze and greasy-cooking smells. Beach got the whiskey bottle off the bunk and helped himself to a pull, but Larkin waved it aside. He had settled his heavy weight onto a corner of the deal table. Mayes, seeing the dark mood on both these men, remained standing—on the defensive.

"All right," he blurted. "So I missed my shot last night. In the light I had it ain't to be wondered at! I could of got him with a second bullet," he added pointedly, "only your wife spoiled my chance—the way she come charging out of the hotel. You wouldn't of wanted me putting a slug into Irene, would you?"

Britt Larkin had stiffened, his craggy face taking on anger. "Leave Irene out of it!" he snapped. "We didn't come to talk about last night—that's over and done, and no help for it now. An old story!"

The other looked sharply at the faces of his visitors, reading hints. "You mean there's more already! What's up? What's happened?"

"Nothing at all—except I been shoved off Dragoon Meadow! Kincaid and the entire Block S crew rode in and took the camp by surprise. Killed two of my men, forced Jack and the others I'd sent up there into helping drive off the stock."

Mayes took this news in stunned silence. His scowl moved to Jack Beach, narrowed there. "Were you asleep, maybe? To let that mongrel crew of Sullivan's——"

"Leave it alone!" growled Beach harshly. Charlie Mayes shrugged.

"Well," he told Larkin, "I won't pretend to be unhappy seeing your hand called! You moved too fast, Britt, helping yourself to that grass—without a word to me about it first. Now you've lost it, we start from scratch again; and this time, let's neither of us try cutting in ahead of the other. Kincaid gives us enough to buck without mistrusting ourselves!"

The Leaning 7 boss heard him out in silence, a stern distaste for this partner on his curving, heavy lips. He took a cigar from his coat pocket, looked at it a moment, stuffed it back again. When he spoke it was to say coldly, "We'll skip that. The point is: how to get rid of Kincaid."

"Simple enough," replied Mayes promptly. "With a bullet. He's no more than human."

"We tried that way. Last night—remember?"

The other's eyes flashed an angry spark. "You said we'd

forget last night! I just didn't draw the high card. A second time, I should have better luck."

"A second time, Kincaid will have been warned to watch the shadows!"

"Hell, he can't watch four ways at once! Maybe," Mayes went on, his voice growing shrill, "you think I ain't able to finish what I start? Give me a couple days to pick my time. My crew and me, we'll take care of him. We'll cut him to ribbons! You won't have to bother, seeing you lack the nerve for this kind of a job. . . ."

Britt Larkin gave him a contemptuous look and a slow shake of the head. "For someone that counts himself brainy, there's nothing much subtle about you, is there? Sure, you can throw your whole crew at Kincaid; likely you can smash him even if you do lose a few men in the process. And then what happens? What about Port Griswold for instance?"

"That tub of grease?" Mayes snorted. "He'll do what he's always done—nothin'!"

"Better not be too sure. The sheriff is a stupid fool— but even with him there's limits to how raw a deal can be. Maybe your way will have to be the one. But it looks to me we better try something else first."

"Such as what?"

"Oh, I'll cook up something. Right now I'm thinking about John Dalhart and the other valley ranchers. We've already got them seeing things the way we want, and they aren't going to be any happier over Sullivan bringing in a hired gunman. It could be our chance to put some real pressure on from that direction."

Mayes considered, eyes narowed. "Worth trying. Maybe one of us better put a bee into Dalhart's ear."

"I think we'll both talk to him." Larkin eased off the table. "Let's meet down in town in a couple of hours and see what we can do about stirring up the animals."

"Suits me," grunted Mayes. "You'll find me at the hotel—in the bar."

Larkin grunted dryly, "Why, where else?" and, throwing a look at his range boss, headed for the door.

Charlie Mayes stood in the opening and watched them

as they rode away through the brush, dropping from sight beyond the dip of the land with only the stain of dust in the air to mark their going.

When they were out of sight Beach muttered, "I'm always glad to get shut of that rat's nest. It smells bad in there!"

His employer said nothing; Beach gave him a quick look noting the expression on Larkin's dark features. "I think you've got some ideas you aren't talkin' about."

"Why tell that guy everything I know," grunted Larkin, "and give him the chance to foul it up for us?" After a moment's silence, while they rode across the empty hills to the easy rhythm of hoofbeats and saddle sounds, he snapped his fingers suddenly. "That kid! There's the answer!"

"Kid? You mean Rooster Adams?"

"You tell me he's sitting in the shack on Dragoon Meadow, where Kincaid put him. It couldn't be handier! We'd have the devil's own time getting at Kincaid direct . . . but through the youngster, now, I think we got a chance!"

He talked as they rode, and the thick-shouldered Beach listened with a thoughtful scowl. "Uh-huh, it just might work," he agreed. "And less risk than goin' directly after a fast gun like Kincaid. If that punk kid gives you trouble," he added viciously, "I'd like the chance to persuade him a little. He made fun of me this morning; I ain't soon forgettin'."

"We'll see," grunted Larkin. "We'll see. . . ."

Some time after this the glint of green in a hilly pocket brought them, by mutual consent, down off the ridge to let their horses water at a seep spring, where there was a growth of willows and cottonwoods. Drawing in, they roused a frightened thrashing in this growth, and a cow and a calf came bursting into view, swerving to cut past the riders and make for open ground.

It was Leaning 7 stock, the calf unbranded though it was weaning-size. The men shared a look, and Britt Larkin said quickly, "Made to order! Get to work!"

Beach was already taking down his lass rope, shaking

out a loop with expert fingers. The roan, a good roping horse, knew its business thoroughly. A mere touch with the spurs sent it lunging forward, cutting in ahead of the calf. The loop spun, shot forward, and dropped.

Within seconds Beach was out of leather and had the calf thrown and trussed and was collecting materials for a fire. Britt Larkin, still in saddle, used his own coiled rope to keep the worried cow at a distance while at the same time he laid a cautious eye on the rims—on the lookout for approaching riders.

Of course any man had the right to put an iron on his own beef whenever he came across it; only, this was no "Leaning 7" that Jack Beach drew with his red-tipped running hair. Hair and flesh sizzled and the blattings of the calf rose to a frenzied climax; and when he took his knee off and flipped the rope free to let it struggle frantically to its feet, a sprawling "Block S" was burned rawly on the animal's trembling hide.

Larkin nodded, grunting approval. "That ought to do it," he said as Beach recoiled his rope and then proceeded to kick out the fire. "We'll let the brand heal over while we wait and see what, if anything, comes of our talk with Dalhart. Tomorrow will be time enough to fetch the sheriff up. . . ."

Later, riding on alone to Leaning 7, Britt Larkin's thoughts reverted again to the subject of his wife; as usual these thoughts put a scowl on his craggy features, and he sat deep in the saddle with his solid bulk giving to the rhythm of the gray under him.

Irene—and Kincaid! Irene hurrying to this man when she saw him fall at the crash of a six-gun . . . and afterward: Irene lingering at his side; letting him place his hand upon her to help her up the step into the buggy; leaning to look back at him, the smile still upon her mouth as she straightened about again when he was gone from sight.

Jealousy was a close companion with Britt Larkin, born afresh at every careless glance his wife bestowed upon another man. That she did not love him, he had come to accept with a species of frustrated rage. Only through wealth, he knew, could he hope to hold her to him; and the blind determination not to lose her had helped to harden his own ruthless ambitions.

But last night . . .

With an habitual gesture he knuckled his misshapen broken nose and felt the rise of fury. It was high irony that he should have taken his wife down to the settlement the very night this stranger was destined to ride into Apache. At least now, he figured, he had his warning. He had learned that Ross Kincaid held at least a potential attraction for his wife—which gave him a double reason for needing Kincaid disposed of.

It was in this mood that Britt Larkin caught sight of the horse, tethered to a mesquite upright of the low gallery fronting the Leaning 7 ranch house. A grulla, unfamiliar to his horseman's eye, bearing no brand; the rigging of the saddle, too, was unfamiliar in this country, hinting of more northern ranges.

A sudden, leaping suspicion stiffened him so that he reined the gray to a halt while sharp and smoldering eyes studied that alien mount and its foreign rigging. Then, deliberately, he rode forward and dismounted, dropping leathers, ducked under the low overhang of the gallery, and strode with his solid step to the open doorway.

There he halted . . . as, across the wide, dim room, his wife and Ross Kincaid broke apart and turned to face him.

Coming from the bright outer sunshine, this cool room with its shuttered windows was a dark place of uncertain outlines. Therefore, Britt Larkin could not swear to what he had seen and what he had not in that first quick moment; he could not say for sure that these two had been locked in an embrace, their arms and mouths tightly joined. But suspicion, that was always keen enough, stabbed him with its sharp spur, seeing guilt in the way they instantly parted as his shadow filled the doorway. Jealous fury leaped in him, twisted hard in his vitals, put a sudden trembling through his limbs.

But he did not obey the wild impulse that wanted to set him pawing at the gun that was strapped to his leg beneath the hang of the coat. Something stopped him—

perhaps the knowledge of who and what this Ross Kincaid was; or perhaps Kincaid's voice that spoke coolly and with no tone of guilt or fear, thus putting some small finger of doubt to quell his suspicions:

"Well, Larkin! I didn't know if there was any point waiting to see you or not."

"No?" Britt Larkin's voice sounded foreign to his own ears under the harsh discipline that he laid upon it to hold it steady. "What d'you think you want with me?"

"Not much. Just something to be put on the record to make sure we all had it straight."

Kincaid came forward, spurs jingling and then muffled briefly as he crossed a bear rug that centered the floor. He stopped a couple of paces from the Leaning 7 boss, thumbs hooked into shell belt and gray stare firm on Larkin's craggy face.

"It's about that business this morning at Dragoon Meadow," he said. "If you're smart, you'll count it closed. Because I'm not going to fool around with you, Larkin; I'm giving it to you straight! Block S is not public graze! If another time I find your cattle on the wrong side of the line, I'm gonna be coming after you—personally. Do I make myself perfectly clear?"

"Why, damn you!" Quick fury sent its fluttering across the big man's tautened cheek muscles. "Get out! Get off this ranch before——"

A wintry smile warped the visitor's thin mouth. "Before what, Britt?" he prompted scornfully. And got no answer.

Turning casually, Kincaid took his Stetson from the chair where he had dropped it on entering the room and sought the woman who stood at the center table yonder. Irene Larkin had one hand against the edge of the table, the other at her white throat.

"Good afternoon, ma'am," he said pleasantly. "I'll be seeing you again."

She made no move and no answer. Britt Larkin knew the swelling of rage within his throat—but there was also the bitter, humiliating taste of fear. He too, therefore, kept silent. And, in this heavy stillness, Ross Kincaid calmly pulled on his big hat and walked from the house.

He passed very close to the other man but without even looking at him, ducked the low lintel and went under the gallery shadow to his waiting horse, flipped the reins loose and swung astride. Erect in the saddle, swaying easily to the movement of the mount, he rode off through the screen of cottonwoods.

Only when he was out of sight did Britt Larkin realize he was holding breath trapped in his lungs. He let this go slowly; flexed fingers that were suddenly stiff and cramped. "Damn him!" he cried in a hoarse outburst. "Damn the——!" But this weak epithet shamed him, and he left it unfinished.

Turning instead, he met his wife's look.

Her eyes were cool, with that faint hint of mute dislike that he had come to recognize in them. Britt Larkin moved a step toward her. "How long was he here?"

"Not long," she answered, and with a shrug she put her back to him and idly opened a book that lay upon the table.

All at once he was at her side, and he found his hand gripping her wrist viciously—forcing her to face him, dragging her against his hard body. A small sound of pain broke from her, but that was all; her eyes, close to his own, merely stared at him in plain contempt.

Britt Larkin could feel the sweat that started upon his forehead; his lips moved on words that wouldn't quite frame themselves. He had the clear, bitter knowledge he was only making himself ridiculous.

"You were in his arms," he cried, goaded past caring. "I saw it. You were kissing——!"

"Let go of me!"

She neither confirmed nor denied; but he knew the truth. Frenzy shook him—passed, leaving only the hard certainty that his rage could not touch this woman at all.

Savagely he thrust her away from him and whirled to stride, beaten, from the room.

Evening settled across this wide land; the saffron stain
left the sky above the crumpled western hills, turned the
inverted bowl of the heavens into silver, darkened the outlines of the rimming earth. Ross Kincaid stood with his
shoulders against a bar of the corral at Sullivan's, savoring
the sour tang of the wind that breathed against him.

It brought with it the occasional ring of iron on stone:
Old Mac, trailing a pack horse laden with supplies, was
riding to join Rooster in his lonely vigil at the Dragoon
Meadow cabin. Then these sounds faded and came no
longer. An aura of peaceful quiet lay upon the Block S as
dusk smoothed and blended the harsh outlines.

At the bunk shack and house, lamplight gleamed softly.
The clatter of tinware sounded as Claire Sullivan went
about cleaning up after the evening meal; turning his head,
Kincaid could see her shadow cross the open doorway as
she moved about between stove and sink.

She never sang as she worked, he reflected. She was
almost as silent in her way as the puncher, George, who
sat alone in the bunk shack now, reading an ages-old, dog-
eared magazine. . . . Kincaid fumbled out a match and
scraped it along the corral pole, cupped it with his hands
as his head bent to bring the flame to his ready cigarette.
Shaking out the match, he turned and walked slowly
toward the house.

He came around the corner as Ward Sullivan stepped
from the door to stand with gaze lifted out across the
deepening darkness of the bench. The crunch of a man's
boots sounded loud in the hush, and big Sullivan swung
his head toward Kincaid as the latter came up and stopped
beside him.

"This stillness gets into a man," said Sullivan. "It goes
to work inside of him and somehow irons out all the hard
knots and leaves him the better for it. You stay up here
long, you'll feel it too."

Kincaid merely grunted, noncommittally. The other asked, "Macready's left for Dragoon Meadow?"

"Some time ago."

"Good! I have to admit, I'll feel better with him there." However, Sullivan had not pressed his new foreman with questions since the latter's return from Leaning 7. He had been content with Kincaid's brief announcement of an understanding with Larkin . . . his statement that, in his opinion, the Dragoon Meadow incident could be considered closed.

Now the older man fought down a yawn and, rising onto his toes with both hands set against the small of his back, stretched tired muscles. "Lord, I do think I'm going to sleep tonight!" he exclaimed. "Reckon I'll pay my respects to Diablo and turn in. It's been a long day."

"You ready to ride that black yet?"

"Almost," said Sullivan. "One of these days. One of these days soon . . ."

Kincaid, about to answer, all at once pulled erect and dropping his cigarette into the dust, set his boot on it. "Riders!" he grunted. "Up the bench trail!"

Himself catching the muffled rhythm of hoofs, Ward Sullivan had turned again to listen. Now he lifted his voice across the quiet of the yard, calling toward the bunkhouse: "George! A light here!"

The riders came on. Kincaid felt for the handle of his sheathed gun, loosening it in the holster. Behind him he heard the tap of Claire Sullivan's heels as she left her work and hurried to the door; and now George was running up from the bunk shack with a lighted lantern. Sullivan took this from him to hang it on a nail beside the door. It laid its light across the group waiting there, but would show the visitors as well.

After that the dark shapes were breaking into the yard, and the feist pup was hustling out to give cry and be sharply silenced. They waited, then, as the horses pulled to a stop and a quick rising of lamp-gilded dust thinned and settled.

Charlie Mayes was there; also Britt Larkin and Jack Beach. The fourth member of the party was a stranger to Kincaid, and he seemed oddly out of place in such com-

pany—a tall, competent figure, ramrod straight in the saddle, with a fine head of snowy hair and trimmed white
whisker, and an altogether aristocratic bearing. Sullivan
murmured in an aside, "That's John Dalhart—the big
rancher on the Apache bottoms." He stepped forward to
greet the white-haired rancher with a reserve that utterly
ignored Dalhart's companions.

"Evening, John! I do believe it's the first time you've
ever favored us with a call. We'd be proud to have you
step down—but not your friends. None of these three is
welcome in my house!"

The redheaded Charlie Mayes stirred angrily but held
his tongue. It was Dalhart who answered, in a deep, slow
Texas voice that contained breeding and a sure self-con-
fidence.

"All I have to say, I can say in a few words, Sullivan—
and it's got nothing to do with the squabbling between
your outfits here on the bench. The Valley has kept its
nose out of this as long as it didn't affect our interests or
our brands."

Sullivan nodded curtly. "Sound policy."

"But now we hear you've gone and hired yourself some
fast-gun artist," Dalhart continued. "And that may or
may not be our business. Where is this man? I want a look
at him."

"You mean my new foreman, Ross Kincaid." Sullivan
stepped aside, jerking his head. "You're looking at him."

"So?" The rancher's stare swung and settled on the lean,
unspeaking stranger who stood beside the Block S boss.
He studied him with a cold interest. "Britt Larkin," he
said finally, "tells me you pulled a raid on one of his camps
this morning, shot up a few of his men. As I said, that's
strictly between yourselves—and the sheriff, if one of you
wants to bring him into it.

"Only, keep your violence and your gunplay up here
on the bench! Sullivan, you've been warned before that
the Valley has its eye on you. If the coming of this Kincaid
is to mean a stepping up in our loss of cattle southward
across the Line, then you're going to bring down on yourself a storm that all the hired guns and jailbird crews you

can scrape together won't save you from! Force our hand, and O'Malley and Ortiz and I will ride up here and clean you off this bench if we have to!"

He ended sharply, "I was elected to pass that word to you. Best remember it—because it's the last warning you're going to get!"

"John——" Sullivan began placatingly, but Kincaid broke in before he could say more.

"Don't plead with him!" Kincaid's voice was hard, his stare corrosive as it swung between the faces of the mounted men. "He's spoken his piece, and he's showed where he stands. Mayes and Larkin have pumped him full, obviously; they've already got him believing whatever they want him to, and it will take more than words to change his mind. So why waste talk?"

John Dalhart had stiffened visibly. "Why indeed?" he snapped. "If I should have to come up here another time, it will be with something stronger than words! And for now, I've no more to say."

Even in anger the old autocrat had lost none of his stern composure. Protocol unforgotten, he touched hatbrim courteously to the girl who stood silent in the doorway. "Good evening, Miss Sullivan," he greeted her. Then he turned his high-stepping black gelding, whose hide glimmered sleekly in the lantern light, and he left there at a rolling lope, heading back down the valley trail.

A grin of open triumph was smeared across Britt Larkin's meaty features as he looked at Sullivan. But, sliding on to Kincaid, his expression warped into hatred. With a savage pull of the reins and thrust of spurs he spun his horse to follow Dalhart and Jack Beach. And Charlie Mayes went with him.

Quickly the yard emptied of horsemen; dust settled again, and the sound of hoofbeats threaded out.

"Better douse this," grunted Kincaid, and, stepping to the wall peg, jacked up the lantern chimney and blew it out, plunging the yard into blackness except for the house and bunk-shack windows. "I've already been shot at once, here, with a light behind me. I don't favor setting myself up for a second try!"

Sullivan spoke, and his voice was solemn. "I wish you hadn't talked to Dalhart quite that way. He's an honest man, and a powerful one; not a man I'd want to deliberately antagonize."

"He graveled me," Kincaid answered briefly. "His smug kind always does. He probably built his herd with a running iron in the days when the range was free and a man could get himself an empire that way. Now that he's rich, wealth has taught him piety. It's always like that."

"In a good many cases," Sullivan agreed reluctantly. "I don't think, though, you'd find a greedy loop in Dalhart's past. If any man was completely honest, I'd say that man was John Dalhart!"

Kincaid shrugged. "You just ain't looked deep enough. A man's rep grows along with him; time he gets up as far as Dalhart, nobody remembers what put him where he is. It's as simple as that!"

Sullivan did not argue the point further. A moment afterward he headed for Diablo's corral. George had already drifted back to his reading in the bunkhouse. Kincaid stood alone a moment longer, looking at the night; then, fumbling for the makin's, he remembered that he was out of matches and turned to the house to get some from the box above the stove.

Claire Sullivan, having finished with the supper dishes, was already commencing another task: she had set a basket of newly laundered clothing upon the trestle table and was sorting through it, with a big flatiron heating on the fire. Kincaid fished out his matches and paused a moment while he transferred them to his shirt pocket, casually leaning his hips against the wall and watching her at work.

Again he noticed the way every movement seemed mechanical, as if she had no interest in what she did. Her back was turned to him, her head bent; he studied the set of her shoulders, saw how her brown hair lay against her fair neck, beneath the cloth she wore about her head. She had a good skin, and her figure was not bad at all. Her features, too, were well shaped, and she could have been pretty if she ever smiled. But not yet had he surprised on her any expression other than a certain hard, sullen rebelliousness.

Kincaid said idly, "A pleasant evening."

She made no answer, did not so much as glance around. Her hands, ignoring his presence, went on with their sorting. And irritation prodded at him.

Scowling, he demanded, "Can't you be civil? Don't you know how to do anything but work?"

At this, she swung about and for the first time gave him her full attention. Her brown eyes were hard with disliking; there was whiteness in the tiny muscles at the corners of her mouth. She snapped, "I was never taught to do anything but work. What kind of teaching did you have?"

Her emotion surprised Kincaid. He looked at her for some moments before he spoke, weighing his answer—remembering what he knew about this girl and the very real hardships and ignominy of her early years, but still not wholly able to excuse her manner, notwithstanding.

"I pretty much taught myself," he said finally, meeting her cold look levelly. "Nobody yet ever had a monopoly on hard luck, Miss Sullivan. I know, because I had my share. Still, I didn't let it sour me against the world completely!"

Her lip curled; her fists were clenched against her thighs. "And why should I be civil?—when all I'd like from you would be to see you ride away from here and leave us alone —before you've brought my father to ruin, or worse!"

"I doubt if your father would agree with that opinion," he reminded her coldly.

"My father is blind in some ways. He knows what you are as well as I do! He knows you're completely cynical and vicious; he heard the way you talked about a man as fine as John Dalhart. And yet he keeps you!" She added fiercely, "You believe there's no good in any man, don't you?"

"That's a little strong, maybe. Put it another way: I figure there's no man who isn't human—which means he's pretty sure to have some bad in him if you look deep enough. That's only common sense!"

Her mouth worked. "You enjoy talking that way, I guess.

Why can't you take the money Dad's already paid you and take your gun and get out?—before your cynicism has destroyed everything we've sacrificed and fought for since the day he left prison?"

As she finished she was fighting to control her breathing. It lifted her breasts under the cheap print cotton of the faded dress, put a suspicious trembling into her tight-pressed lips. But her eyes held Kincaid's, angry and defiant.

"I wonder," he said then, slowly, his voice speculative. "Is it really me you're so afraid of—or maybe something else you're scared you might find inside? You fancy yourself for a pretty cold potato. But supposing, now, that a man was to——"

A brash impulse sent him toward her, his hands seizing her and discovering in the warm flesh of her arms a softness at variance with her cold and brittle manner. But then, before his lips could find hers, she had recovered from shocked surprise and was tearing loose from his hands, and her arm lifted and her palm raked him across the cheek.

There was nothing gentle in that slap. Claire Sullivan put weight into it, and it staggered him. Then, whirling, she saw the heavy iron heating on the stove, and she snatched it up, lifted it threateningly between them as she backed away.

Her face was white with fury; her teeth showing between tight-pulled lips. She whispered hoarsely, "You touch me again! You just dare to put a finger on me . . ."

Involuntarily he had lifted a hand to his stinging cheek. He stood like that a moment, eying her, his look holding no emotion beyond surprise at her violent reaction. Then, abruptly, Ross Kincaid turned and walked out of the house, this picture of her filling his mind.

And anger—and a kind of shame—went with him.

Later he sat on the bench in front of the bunkhouse and had his thoughts. The feist ranch pup, that had long since made friends with him, came and jumped up beside him and gave his face a dab or two with its tongue; then curled into a tight ball, nose to tail. Kincaid scratched the stubby hairs along its back, frowning at the run of his reflections.

His thoughts were of women. Lonely as the trail had been, he was not without experience of them; and they were perverse creatures—either all fire or all ice—and none of them as easily manageable as male pride was wont to suppose. Twice today he had had a woman in his arms, for fleeting moments, yet he knew little more of these two than he had guessed before.

There was more of the ice than of the fire in both of them . . . yet with a deep difference: Claire Sullivan's was the chill hostility of a woman who wants nothing from life and will accept nothing; Irene Larkin's, the cool sureness that wants much and will accept it from any likely source. Thus they actually were worlds apart—and increasingly interesting as you knew them. For the Sullivan girl was no drab, however much life had spoiled her. And as for Irene . . .

His thought turned to her. Yes, she was cool enough and sure enough of herself—even if she made an occasional mistake, as she had been frank to admit in discussing Britt Larkin that afternoon in the Leaning 7 ranch house. Kincaid knew now that she had come to Larkin on the rebound from the death of a former husband: a man considerably older than herself—an adventurer of sorts apparently—who had showered easy wealth upon her and then, with his sudden ending, left her penniless and stranded by chance in a western cattle-market town. Under such circumstances, and desperate as she was, it had been no trick for Larkin to sell himself to her; disillusionment had come later, and it had been bitter indeed.

And now she had seen the arrival of a stranger; and already Ross Kincaid had held her in his arms and felt the response of her lips against his own. There had been little passion in the kiss, but it was one he would remember. He would remember, too, the expression on her husband's face as he stood in the doorway! Kincaid smiled a little in the darkness; but he knew this was not really a matter for amusement.

And what did Irene Larkin want from him? He hadn't any illusions about that, either; or so he told himself. Kincaid represented to her a chance of escape from this bleak land and from the boor who held her prisoner. Anyone else who offered escape would be equally agreeable just now. Yet the fact remained that she was a highly desirable woman—and that she would undoubtedly be very grateful, for a time at least, to the man who helped get her what she wanted. . . .

Kincaid shrugged and rose. The lights had gone out in house and bunk shack. He told the pup, "Well, I got saddle work ahead of me tonight—and more important things to think about than a couple of females!"

No woman had ever interfered with his efficiency . . . no woman, by Kincaid's lights, was worth it.

VIII   ACTION BY NIGHT

At the bunkhouse doorway he paused, thinking the lonely chore he had picked for himself was one that a pair could handle better. But the seldom-speaking George would be little company, and, besides, he had not yet been cleared of the distrust in which Kincaid held most men, even though he had done his part in the showdown at Dragoon Meadow. George could too easily prove to be a border hopper himself. At any rate he had his secrets, and it wasn't with such a man that Kincaid elected to ride this dangerous border graze alone.

So he passed him up, leaving him asleep in the darkened bunk shack, and moved on to the night corral, where the grulla waited, rested now from its workout during the day. He got his gear and had the horse saddled when a footfall sounded near him, and Ward Sullivan's voice asked quietly, "Traveling, Kincaid?"

He spun, startled, to find the rancher close beside him. For just an instant came the hard suspicion that Sullivan might have learned about that scene with Claire and thought that he was sneaking flight rather than face the consequences. Angry, the girl's father might make almost any reckless move.

Ross Kincaid put a hand on the butt of his holstered gun. "I was thinking," he answered carefully, "I'd take a little ride and have a look at those southern hills. Britt Larkin is a fast-acting gent, to judge from the way he put a trap for us at Dragoon before we expected. Now that they've heard Dalhart lay out the law to us, he and Mayes are pretty certain to step up their raids and give the ranchers cause to throw their whole force at us and smash us. I think it's a good hunch that cattle are going to be moving—tonight!"

"I see," murmured Sullivan thoughtfully. "Yes, I see what you mean."

Relief went through Kincaid then, and he dropped his hand from the gun. Sullivan didn't know about that scene in the ranch house. Somehow, Kincaid hadn't thought that Claire would tell.

"You're thinking," Sullivan went on, "that you can cut in on those raiders . . . maybe even break up a play for them? Rooster has sometimes talked like that, but Mac and I always voted him down. There's too few of us. Besides, Dalhart would only need to catch one Block S man night riding down there to settle forever any doubts he still may have."

Kinkaid nodded impatiently. "I've considered that. Still, I'm not Rooster Adams. I figure to take care of myself. And, after all, until we know how those crooks operate we can hardly do anything about stopping them. So I'm riding."

"All right." Sullivan sounded resigned but unconvinced. "I should never question your judgment—I've found out that you always have your reasons. Give me a minute. I'll get my horse."

"I'm a younger man than you," Kincaid protested quickly. "I can skip a little sleep, now and then, and make it up. You're dead tired; I don't think you'd better buy into this."

But the other insisted doggedly. "I'll ask no man to take a needless risk. I know that country, while you've never seen it even by daylight. If we run into anything, I could maybe save you the cost of a bad mistake."

Kincaid thought it over. "That makes sense, I guess," he admitted. And Sullivan set quickly to work.

The night had turned darker with a thin cloud drift that smothered out the stars; there would be no moon until nearly morning. The small wind that walked the shadowed earth made sounds deceptive and uncertain, so that they rode cautiously as their horses picked out the trail down to lower country.

They took their time approaching the fording of the creek but found nothing here that spelled danger; so they crossed, and then Kincaid dismounted to check for sign by the flicker of a palm-sheltered match.

"Pretty fresh tracks," he muttered. "A bunch of them. Somebody's been through here ahead of us."

"Wouldn't that be Dalhart and the others?"

"Maybe. Though Dalhart would more probably be alone—no good reason for Larkin or Mayes to have ridden back to Apache with him. . . . Let's play it this way, for a while anyhow." He mounted again, and they struck southward across rolling graze, alert to movement in the night since they must count this bottom land as enemy country. Ahead, the fishhook curve of the hills bulked ever nearer.

The land became more uneven as they proceeded, more cut up with spurs thrust out by the barren roughs. They left the better graze, hit stretches of outcrop where their shoe irons struck sparks from naked rock. Finally, at the foot of the wall, Kincaid called a halt to consider and let their horses have a rest.

Only now did he begin to see the full size of the job he had lightly taken on. As Sullivan had remarked, the hills were as full of holes as a sieve. In a ten-mile stretch, there must be at least a hundred open draws into which cattle could disappear, a few head at a time . . . altogether too many for a pair of men to check on in a single moonless night.

"Now I understand," he muttered, "why there's been no luck stopping this business. A smart crook could sneak through any patrols the Valley men sent out. To Larkin and Charlie Mayes, it must look like a made-to-order setup."

The other man hesitated an instant. "If we're sure," he said, "it's them doing it."

Kincaid glanced at him, surprised. "You have any doubts?"

"Not many. Still, I've blamed Dalhart for believing in a man's guilt without evidence; I'd hate to do the same myself. It would clear my own mind if I just once saw actual proof!"

"Well, maybe we'll get you some!" Kincaid spoke gruffly, impatient and yet respectful of the older man's meticulous honesty—his reluctance to condemn on mere suspicion.

He said, changing the subject, "Sound rises. Let's hunt us some high point and try a lookout from there, just on the chance . . ."

"Good idea."

A ridge spur gave them the vantage they wanted. They ascended its rugged flank, picking a way through brush and outcrop, then dismounting to tie their horses while they moved into a position commanding the whole wide sweep of range land. The night could hardly have been blacker, thanks to the star-obscuring haze that piled the shadows up. A chilly wind pushed against them, whipped at mesquite that clung to the barren rock; it brought no other sounds.

Kincaid put a long, intent survey on that void gaping at his feet, swinging his attention in a slow arc that missed no possible sight or sound. Ward Sullivan, waiting, grew impatient. "We're wasting time," he said finally, his voice sounding loud after the silence. "There's not a thing stirring. We better be getting down from here and moving farther east——"

"Quiet!" the other rapped sharply. Sullivan broke off, listening, but still heard nothing.

"It sounded like a steer bawling," Kincaid explained. "I'm easing down for a look. You stay here—one of us will make less noise than two."

Not waiting for argument, he was quickly in saddle and picking his way down the scattered slope, pausing at its foot as he keened the wind for a repetition of the sound he wasn't entirely sure he had heard.

The rattle of brush around him covered anything. If it had been a steer, it might only be some stray, lonesome in the breaks or startled by a prowling animal. Kincaid ticked steel to flank and sent the grulla cautiously ahead, every nerve tensed in a trained alertness.

All at once a shifting in the wind brought it strongly—the unmistakable mutter of cattle being moved against their will . . . and, once, the quick piercing clang of iron on stone.

He pulled rein, an instinctive jerk of the wrist. To his right was the black mouth of a draw apparently slicing deep into the hills; it was, he knew suddenly, the goal of those nearing beef animals. The gun slid into Kincaid's fingers with the faint whisper of oiled metal against leather. And he was spurring the grulla forward, putting it into the shadows lying thick a few yards within and to one side of the draw's opening.

After that he waited, six-gun leveled across saddle swell.

There was more sound now, drawing steadily nearer. It resolved itself into the slough of hoofs, the clack of clashing horns, the bawling of a protesting steer. A man's voice, small in the night, called out something . . . another answered.

A couple riders, maybe more; possibly a score of steers. And very close now.

Kincaid thumbed the hammer spur, rocked it back with a sharp click. His hand was steady enough on the gun, and he noted this with half of his mind, and was pleased.

His controls were still there; some day, he supposed, in some such spot as this there would be an uneasy reluctance that would put its queasiness into his belly and cause his palm to sweat against the butt plates of a Colt. Then he would know that he had taken enough and that his career as a gun fighter was at an end. But the time was not yet, and danger still held its cool exhilaration and not fear. . . .

Suddenly, almost explosively, moving shapes took form against the dark night curtain, and the first of the stolen steers was upon him—almost under the grulla's nose. He felt their nearness, heard the snort of wind through nostrils, smelled the hides and the dust lifted by plodding hoofs. Still he waited, and presently came the familiar creak of gear and jingle of bit chains and a rider showed dimly, almost upon him. Kincaid slowly raised the gun.

Then the grulla under him, catching near scent of another horse, swelled its sides and loosed a shrill whicker of greeting.

He cursed silently; but the damage was done. Yards distant, that other rider pulled to an abrupt stop. There was a startled gasp, and the man's voice, strained and tense, cried, "What is it? Who's there, damn it?"

On the tail of the words a blossom of gun flame exploded; Kincaid thought he almost felt the sear of its heat. His own ready finger tripped trigger, the two shots mingling. And as the blackness clamped down again a hoarse cry told him he had scored a hit.

Amid yells, other guns were opening up—a pair of them. Kincaid might have retreated into cover somewhere within the draw; he did not even think of it. Instead he slammed in the steel and sent his grulla plunging straight forward, his own gun answering.

The grulla swerved as the horse whose saddle he had emptied came lunging across his path.

Then frightened, bellowing steers were around him, shouldering his mount. Once he felt it thrown off stride, barely saved himself a spill with a yank at the reins that helped the grulla come out of it. And through all this he was triggering fast at the flash of the guns opposite.

It was a wild, confused moment. Kincaid drove ahead against the stream of cattle, refusing to give ground. The audacity of his charge had its effect. Expecting no trouble and instead running into accurate gunfire that had dropped one of them from saddle, his opponents were not prepared for a real fight. Likely they were not even sure if one man or half a dozen had laid this trap for them. Their return fire lasted only seconds; then they were turning tail and striking off across the broken flats and scattering fast.

Kincaid let them go, hauling in while he reloaded. Pursuit, he knew, would be useless. Instead he was turning back when a quick run of hoofbeats bearing from the west pulled him quickly that way, the smoking gun tipping up again in his hand.

But then he guessed what this meant and held his fire, calling, "Sullivan? It's all right."

His boss was beside him, panting and excited. "I hit saddle the instant I heard firing start. I couldn't know what you had run into!"

"Dropped one; the others took off." Kincaid added, "Don't know whether the man I shot is alive or dead. Take a look, will you, while I round up his bronc before it gets away."

He wheeled and spurred into the draw, whooping to scatter such few remaining steers as had not already broken away under the gunfire. The sides of the draw, closing in, beat back echoes of the grulla's hoofs as Kincaid took after the vanished horse.

When he returned minutes later, he had its reins anchored to his saddle horn and was chousing three steers ahead of him to the swing and slap of his coiled rope. Sending them north across the flats, he reined over to where Sullivan hunkered at the mouth of the draw and there dismounted.

"Dalhart cattle, all right," he grunted. "They wore the J-D Connected iron. The brand on the horse had been covered with pitch, but I scraped it off. Want to guess how it reads?"

"I already know," Sullivan answered in a strange voice. "A 'Star.' This man you shot is one of Charlie Mayes' riders —fellow name of Blondy Hill."

"Alive?" Kincaid wanted to know quickly.

"Barely."

Squatting on his heels, Kincaid examined the wounded rustler by the light of the match his boss thumbed to life. Sullivan had done what he could but that was little enough; the bullet had taken Blondy Hill through the body, doing terrible damage inside. Black blood pulsed from the gaping wound; blood was on his lips, where ragged breathing formed bubbles of reddish spittle. Ward Sullivan tried to keep it wiped away with a soggy bandanna.

The dying man turned his head a little, blurred eyes focusing on the match glow. Kincaid demanded sternly, "You hear me, Blondy?"

"Doctor . . ." the broken voice mumbled. "Get me . . . doctor."

"Sorry, Blondy. No doctor could patch that up."

"I'm gonna die?" The wavering stare found his face. The yellow-haired man was not much more than a youngster—only a few years past Rooster's age, probably—but there was hardness in him. "Damn you!" he gritted, his face twisting in a spasm of pain. "You done it to me! You're . . . Kincaid —ain't you?"

"I'm Kincaid. And you and those others were running a jag of Dalhart beef across to Mexico for your boss. You been doing that pretty often?"

The lips quirked defiantly. "Often enough . . . damn you!" The defiance was lost in a quick grimace of pain.

"Listen to me!" snapped Kinkaid, bringing the man's stare back to him as it began to waver. "And answer when you're talked to! Mayes isn't alone in this business, I take it. Britt Larkin's a part of it too?"

"Hell with you!" grunted the dying man thickly. "Sure, Larkin's in on this. You think Charlie ever had brains enough for——"

A convulsion seized him, twisted his face unrecognizably, dropped him limp. Slowly the match in Sullivan's hand burnt down to a blackened twist and went out.

Kincaid straightened. "Well," he said, gruffly, "there's the proof you wanted! I guess there aren't any doubts left in your mind now."

"Hardly!" Ward Sullivan sounded a little shaken by this experience with death. "If only the sheriff could have heard . . ."

"But he didn't. So we've just got to be satisfied with having our private guesses confirmed."

"Yes. At least there's that." Sullivan placed both hands on bent knees, stiffly pushed himself erect. "And now?"

The pressure of Kincaid's hand and Kincaid's quick word of warning silenced him. On indrawn breaths both of them listened, and now Sullivan, too, got it: the unmistakable sound of running horses, fast nearing!

Sullivan exclaimed, "I wasn't the only one heard that shooting!"

"Well, it's certain we can't afford to be caught here! Let's move. . . ."

Kincaid himself was in leather without any waste of time, throwing loose the reins of Blondy's horse. Ward Sullivan's mount, however, was making trouble: it had caught the scent of blood on his hands and was circling at reins' end, snorting its fear as he tried vainly to gain the stirrup. Kincaid, seeing what was wrong, slammed his grulla against the animal and held it steady until his boss could lift himself astride.

After that they used the steel and had their mounts lined out at a hard run. There was only small leeway. Mere seconds behind them a clot of horsemen came pouring in across the dark flats. A gun winked; the slap of sound drew an oath from Kincaid, knowing from this that they had indeed been sighted.

Quickly the thing had shaken down into a chase, streaming westward along the fringe of hills. However, despite this narrowness of pursuit, they had to curb their speed since any misstep, on such treacherous ground, could mean death to a running horse and its rider both. Twisting once in saddle, Kincaid found his Colt in his hand and holstered it with an angry thrust—chagrined at the impulse that would prompt him to empty his gun now in useless firing when at any moment he might want a full cylinder.

The pursuers observed no such caution. Spurred by the seeming chance of closing this bag on a pair of cattle thieves, they were shooting but shooting wild. And steadily they were thinning down the distance.

Then the ground dropped breathlessly from under Kincaid, and man and horse went spilling into a pileup. He tried in desperation to kick free, failed entirely to clear the stirrups. The full weight of the grulla, descending squarely upon one leg, pinned him under.

Yet, as by a kind of miracle, a soft, cushioning bed of loose silt received his fall. Stunned, he had presence of mind enough to fling both arms about his head as the grulla thrashed and scrambled to its feet; one shod hoof grazed his forearm but did no worse than that, and the instant his trapped leg was free, he was rolling aside and pawing his way out of the soft drift, hearing Sullivan's anxious cry close at hand. He panted reassurance.

It was a dry and silted stream bed into which he had tumbled; Sullivan's mount had managed the drop safely. Limping after his horse, Kincaid felt for holster and was relieved to find the gun intact. By the time he had snagged the grulla's flying reins and flung himself astride again, the thunder of pursuit was very close indeed. But now he had also settled on a way of escape.

He snapped an order, and, swinging the grulla, headed him in a new course down the throat of the dry bed. His companion, evidently sensing that Kincaid must have a plan, followed without question. Silt clung to the horses' hoofs and slowed them as under the spurs they plunged forward. Branches of scrub willow that lined the shallow banks reached to brush the riders' shoulders.

Perhaps a hundred feet on Kincaid abruptly pulled rein and set the grulla to crowding Sullivan, shoving the other's mount back in under the willows. "Keep him quiet!" he ordered tersely. "This is likely our one chance. . . ."

Already horsemen were pouring into the dry bed. A voice they both recognized as John Dalhart's was yelling for a halt: Every word came clearly across the darkness as he cannily pointed out, "It's a trick! I don't hear their horses!"

"They're trying to throw us off," someone suggested, "by cutting into this arroyo. The silt muffles them."

"Then look for sign. And hurry it!"

"Who's got a light?"

Seconds later came the quick shout of triumph: "What did I tell you? Straight into the gulley . . ."

Like hounds on the scent, that cavalcade came pouring then, strung out by the narrowness of the channel. Muffled in deep drift, their hoofs made only a whisper of sound—less noise than the labored breathing of the mounts or the grunt a rider gave when a low-swaying willow frond slapped at him.

The pair waiting in concealment felt the growing pulse of tension as the horsemen drew abreast of their hiding spot . . . and suddenly they were streaming past, near enough that a man almost could have reached and touched them. When they were gone, Kincaid slowly lowered the gun he had held ready, let trapped wind from his lungs.

"Close!" he muttered. "And we're not done yet. Sooner or later Dalhart will tumble to the fact there's nobody out in front of him. Before he does, and turns back, we'll have to make distance."

"And with our tracks buried," Sullivan added, "so that they can't trail us home."

"No problem in such country." Kinkaid spoke shortly; his leg was paining him now where the grulla had rolled on it, and he had no liking for this hare-and-hounds business.

Impatiently he set about hunting a way up the crumbling side of the arroyo. On the second try he made it, the grulla scrambling to solid ground. And a moment later Ward Sullivan joined him.

"All right?" Kincaid waited for the other's grunt of assurance.

They struck out at a long, reaching gait, then pointed toward the crossing of Apache Creek. Quickly the black night swallowed them.

IX   TORTURE METHODS

The sky was brassy, cloudless, the morning already turning out unpleasantly warm; the sheriff, following Jack Beach up the narow shelving trail to Leaning 7, made heavy going of it. His gross bulk swayed to the plodding of the big-boned sorrel. He had one fleshy hand clamped over the pommel to hold him balanced in leather, and in the other he carried a wadded blue handkerchief with which he constantly swabbed the greasy perspiration from his face and wattled throat, reaching far under the collar and puffing as he did it.

He said, "I wish to hell you'd let me in on the secret. What's it all about?"

The foreman looked back at him across a hulking shoulder. "Larkin said fetch you. He'll tell you himself, quick enough."

Port Griswold let it go, too unhappy to waste breath in talk. He figured it would be something important or Britt wouldn't have hauled him out and brought him up here. Britt was too intelligent a man. Britt wouldn't send anyone on a wild goose chase. . . .

Still heat lay over the ranch buildings as they came into sight of them. Leaves of the tall cottonwoods hung without stirring; sunlight beat back dazzlingly from the mirror of whitewashed adobe.

They didn't go to the house. The sound of approaching hoofs brought Larkin from the door, and he waved them on toward the corrals and started walking that way himself. He met them beside a pen that held a single cow and calf.

"Good morning, Sheriff," he said briefly.

Port Griswold noded and shoved his Stetson back on his head with a broad thumb; the hatband stuck to his forehead briefly. "Well," he said in a cross voice, "I come with him. Now, what's the ruckus? What did you want to show me?"

For answer, Britt Larkin merely jerked a thumb toward the pen behind him. The sheriff shifted in the hull and stared with a muddled perplexity at the little calf nuzzling hungrily at its mother. Then, seeing the brands, his eyes widened as understanding slowly grew in him. He switched his glance to the rancher quickly, asking a question.

Larkin noded. "That's right. That's just what you see. It's enough, I reckon, to justify a man in anything he wanted to do about it—only, I'm a law-abiding man, Sheriff! This is in your province, and I want you to handle it. I haven't even shown this to my crew, knowing how they were likely to react. They're out on the range now, and they won't be in for hours. You've got a free hand."

The sheriff wiped his forehead again with the soggy rag; suddenly his face seemed without color, and his hand trembled a little. "That—that's fine!" he stammered. "Of course. We'll have to do something, naturally."

A sneer touched the foreman's hard mouth. "What's the matter, Port? You ain't afraid, are you?"

"Shut up!" snapped Larkin, spearing Beach with a threatening look.

Color had seeped back into the sheriff's greasy face. "I've

got to have more facts," he told Jack Beach coldly. "Where did you find this misbranded calf? Do you have any idea who did the job?"

"Of course I do," said Larkin. "I saw it done. It was that Rooster Adams kid."

"Him?" The sheriff's relief was plainly visible. He had no fear of Rooster. "Well, that makes a difference—you havin' seen it, I mean," he explained quickly.

"Mind, I never actually seen him put the iron on the calf. But I come across the place just after he rode away from it. Yesterday afternoon, it was—by a seep spring over north a bit. The ashes of the branding fire were still hot. It was Rooster, all right. Not a doubt of it."

Port Griswold nodded slowly. "I guess there isn't. We've always wanted proof against that Block S crowd; it looks like we've got it now—though that boy is the last one of the lot I'd have expected to be arresting. I always kind of liked the kid; but he wouldn't ride for a man like Sullivan, I reckon, if there was any decency in him. It just shows how a crook like that can take a youngster and corrupt him. . . ." His massive shoulders lifted heavily. "Well, I reckon I'll have to make an arrest."

"It shouldn't be too hard," Larkin told him. "He's holding down the Dragoon Meadow shack, all by himself; just a matter of riding over and picking him up. I'd like to go along, if you don't mind."

"That's all right. As the accusing witness I'll want you with me."

"I'm ready to ride. . . ."

And he was, at that, with the gray saddled and waiting at the corral gatepost. In a matter of minutes he was mounted and placing himself at the sheriff's side, heading toward Block S grass. Nobody had mentioned Jack Beach's coming, but he put his own horse behind the other pair, and Port Griswold appeared to have no objections. They rode in silence, as though they all were stirred by the grimness of their errand.

Rooster must have sighted them the instant the trio of riders came across a barren ridge. The door of the shack burst open and he flung himself at the corral fence where his pony was tied, making a hurriedly desperate effort to get the cinches tightened and himself into leather before they could overtake him. Seeing this, they spurred their mounts and went in at a rush; and Port Griswold yelled, "Hold it, kid! Stay where you are! This is the law!"

The boy turned then, slowly, and crooked one skinny arm to shade his eyes while he stared at the approaching riders. They halted in a half circle, ringing him against the corral poles, and with hands hooked in gun belt, now, Rooster Adams scowled and said, "Well?" in an uncertain tone.

"I want you to come down to town with me, boy," said Port Griswold in a gruff voice that was not unkindly.

"With you? I can't do it, Sheriff. I got orders to stay here."

"These are new orders. I'm sorry. I got to take you."

Rooster's brick-red face altered; his head jerked exactly as though he had been struck. He ran a wild, hard look across the three riders, ending with Jack Beach who was idly shaping a cigarette. He demanded harshly, "What kind of a Leanin' 7 frame-up is this?"

"No frame-up," said the sheriff stiffly. "You're accused of misbranding one of Britt Larkin's calves to a Block S yesterday afternoon. Larkin himself is the witness."

"Then he's a liar! I never put the wrong iron on any critter, not ever—and since yesterday morning I been sitting right here at this cabin, like Ross Kincaid ordered me!"

"You can prove that, maybe?" said Larkin heavily.

The boy whirled on him. "You know I can't. That's why you figure you can get away with this rigged deal!"

Port Griswold looked troubled. The sagging folds of his throat stirred as he shifted his weight in the saddle. "If you're innocent, you'll have a chance to tell your side. But we're getting nowhere, like this. You've got to go down with me."

"Not a chance!" cried Rooster, his voice near to breaking. "I'm not leavin' this shack. I promised Mr. Kincaid——"

"Kincaid!" grunted Larkin. And he turned to the sheriff, a thoughtful expression carefully concealing his real feelings.

"I dunno, Griswold. As you say, he's only a youngster, and if he's taken a wrong turn it's bad example that's done it. Maybe if I could talk to him a little?" He looked around, then indicated the line cabin with a jerk of his head. "Come inside with me, kid. Maybe we can straighten this out."

"I got nothin' to talk to you about!" Rooster began hotly.

But Britt Larkin was already stepping from the saddle, and the sheriff ponderously followed suit. "This sun out here is pretty hot," Griswold admitted. "Palavering is better in the shade." By now Jack Beach had also dismounted and the three of them were waiting; and, helplessly, Rooster turned and let them herd him toward the shack.

But in the doorway Larkin turned to bar the sheriff from entering. "Lemme talk to him alone, Sheriff," he murmured. "Just a couple of minutes. I might even drop charges if he'll listen to reason."

He shut the door before Port Griswold had a chance to argue; and then he turned to the boy—alone, now, in that shack with the two Leaning 7 men. Jack Beach had set his shoulders against the edge of the door and was putting a match to his cigarette, eying Rooster above cupped hands. Larkin's whole face and manner had changed, gone quickly cruel and mean.

"All right, you!" he gritted. "Now we're gonna stop foolin'——"

Rooster read the evil in his eyes and was suddenly backing away, pawing for the gun thrust into his belt. But Larkin moved too fast for him and, knocking the youngster's hand aside, seized the gun and tossed it across the room onto a bunk. His fingers gripped Rooster's bony shoulder, ground into the flesh.

"You're gonna listen to me, and listen close!" With a shove, he propelled the boy into a rickety chair beside the table that filled most of the room. "You ever see the inside of Yuma Prison?"

Rooster swallowed once, staring into the battered features, the wicked little eyes thrust so near his own. He tried to speak but could not, and shook his head.

"You wouldn't like it," the other went on. "It ain't nice in there—damned cold and cheerless; really too bad for a kid as young as you to end up in such a place. But, by God, that's exactly where I'm going to put you unless you listen to a little sense and do what I tell you!"

Still the boy said nothing, but the fear showed itself in his face that had lost its color, and in the wild eyes, and in the sweat that beaded his beardless upper lip. His mouth trembled a little, and then he steadied it.

Britt Larkin straightened, thick chest swelling. His craggy hands tightened into fists. Boring into his victim with a hard and threatening stare, he gave his ultimatum. "I want you to turn evidence. That's all you have to do, and I'll let you go. Just tell the sheriff Ross Kincaid ordered you to misbrand that calf. . . ."

"Damn you!" shrilled Rooster, stung to sudden fury that swamped his fear. "No! I won't do it. I'm no Judas . . . you can't make me!"

His vehemence rather startled Larkin, who had expected nothing like this. For a moment the man could only scowl, his attack blunted by surprise; then his mouth hardened. "Don't be so sure——"

With an impatient grunt, Jack Beach came striding forward. He rounded the table, moving behind the chair where the youngster crouched in apprehension. Suddenly a vicious swipe of his open palm batted Rooster's hat from his head. Grabbing the boy by his shock of sandy hair, Beach hauled his head sharply back until he was looking straight up into the foreman's glaring eyes.

"You really think we can't make you?"

"You both go to hell!" cried Rooster in a strangled voice.

Cruel pleasure glinted in Jack Beach's eyes, quirked his wide mouth. Very deliberately he took the cigarette from his mouth; he glanced at the glowing end of it and showed it to the prisoner. It was so close that Rooster could feel its heat. The youngster frowned at it, and again at Jack Beach —and, in the man's stare, read his purpose.

But before he could make any move or try to escape, Larkin's foreman had crooked his elbow tight, clamping Rooster's head firmly against the sweaty shirt. And, holding him so, Beach started drawing his cigarette slowly and deliberately toward the prisoner's wide and terror-striken eyes.

Rooster watched it come, his throat and lungs swelled tight, then burst into a sudden frantic scream. "No! No! No!" All at once he was fighting the iron grip that held him powerless, kicking and struggling in utter panic. Spittle flecked his lips.

"Let him go!" growled Larkin suddenly.

Plainly reluctant, Jack Beach loosed his hold and stepped away. Rooster dropped back into the chair, limp and white of face. But when his wild gaze crossed Britt Larkin's, it hardened and took on a firmness that was remarkable after what he had just endured.

"Go on!" he panted. "Burn my damned eyes out! I won't turn traitor, you hear me?—or swear to your filthy lies about Kincaid. . . ."

The door thrust open; Sheriff Griswold brought his heavy weight into the cabin. He stood and blinked about him in vague alarm. "What was all that yelling? What's happenin' here?"

Britt Larkin shrugged. Thwarted fury at Rooster's stubbornness was boiling within him, but he held it from his voice.

"Nothin', Sheriff. The boy and I had a talk. He's sorry for what he done, and he promises he'll never try it again. So—I'm withdrawing charges. We'll just forget about the calf."

"But——" Obviously dissatisfied, Port Griswold turned to the youngster. "This right, kid? What do you say about it?"

Rooster stared back at him for a long moment. He was rumpled, sweat soaked; his thin chest was labored with breathing, and now the sheriff saw a violent tremor run through his body, convulsing him. The hulking figure of Jack Beach stood just behind his chair, and Griswold was positive it was the boy's scream he had heard not two minutes before. Yet if he expected Rooster to lodge a protest against his treatment at the hands of these men, it wasn't forthcoming.

The youngster merely shook his head and said sullenly, in a voice that sounded hardly under control, "It's . . . like he said, I reckon."

"But——" The sheriff's bewilderment carved itself deeper into his flabby face as he tried to square what he had seen and heard with what these people chose to tell him.

Still, there was obviously nothing more to be had out of them. The boy had lapsed into a sullen silence, meeting the sheriff's look unyieldingly. And now Britt Larkin said harshly, "I guess you've had your ride for nothing, Sheriff. But you'll likely agree this way is better than sendin' a kid to the pen; and there's no doubt in my mind but what he'll keep his promise. . . ."

The sheriff gave up, then, with a shrug of his ponderous shoulders. "All right," he grunted. "I just hope it's the last I hear of this. I don't like such business."

"No better'n I do. Well, let's hit saddle. You'll have grub at Leaning 7 with us, naturally. Time enough then to head back."

Larkin seemed suddenly impatient to be off. He was at the door, motioning to his foreman with a jerk of the head. Beach gave the boy in the chair a last, sour look, and he stubbed out the cigarette on the table and flipped it into a corner before turning to shuffle out of the room.

Now Larkin stood waiting, his eye on the sheriff. The latter turned and walked over to him, but at the last minute hesitated for a final look at Rooster. He got nothing, however, but the same cold, impenetrable stare. Giving it up, Port Griswold let Larkin usher him out of the cabin.

After they had gone, Rooster Adams didn't move for a long minute; then the sound of their horses starting brought him out of his chair and to the window, and through the streaked pane he watched them ride away. Suddenly a bitter oath tore from the boy, and one bony fist, clenching, hammered blindly at the edge of the sash.

But helpless fury passed, leaving him sick, and limp, and trembling. Going shakily to the bunk, he picked up his gun, looked blankly at it, shoved it into waistband. His palm was greasy with sweat, and he wiped it along his jeans, then ran a sleeve across his face. The cold perspiration was pouring from him, turning his clothing damp and clammy. His eye chanced to light on the black spot on the table edge where Jack Beach had stubbed out his cigarette, and he jerked away hurriedly as the sight brought quick nausea rising in him.

"Someday!" he gritted in a paroxysm of grief and rage. "Someday, Jack Beach . . ."

He was only lying to himself, of course. He would never be tough enough to settle this with Jack. Just the same, he was resolved to tell no man the truth of what had happened in the Dragoon Meadow shack; not Sheriff Griswold—not even old Mac. Because if he did, the story was bound eventually to reach the ears of Ross Kincaid—and somehow he knew very surely that then Kincaid would kill Beach.

And it was Rooster's score. If he couldn't manage to take his own vengeance, he'd be damned before he'd let another do it for him.

There was, after all, the hard core of bitter pride, and it was all he had—the pride of having stood under the threat of torture, refusing the betrayal it had been meant to force upon him. And yet pride was hardly enough. In that bleak hour it was small comfort, indeed, to Rooster Adams. . . .

Once more the sun was in his face when Ross Kincaid awoke. He told himself, with wry amusement, This job is upsetting my regular hours! He would have liked to have been lazy for once, but Sullivan could ill afford the wages he was being paid; and also, an idea had occurred to him on waking, and he was anxious to act upon it. Accordingly he rose, dressed, and went out into the sunlight that already held the beginnings of strong morning heat. His leg, hurt in that tumble the night before, did not much pain him now.

Ward Sullivan was up ahead of him; over by the corral he and George were reassembling the running gear of an old buckboard that had just undergone needed repairs. Kincaid strolled over to watch and to return Sullivan's greeting; George, absorbed in the work, gave him no more than a glance and a curt nod.

Kincaid, leaning an elbow against a corral pole, inquired casually, "Do we have any bob wire around the place?"

"Wire?" Sullivan looked surprised. "That stuff's too expensive for my bankroll! I'd like to fence my range, sure —but I couldn't afford even a start."

"My idea wouldn't take more than a single spool," Kincaid told him, "and it seems a good investment."

"Let's hear it."

"Why, what I had in mind was a stout, four-strand fence thrown across that gap that opens south from Dragoon Meadow. It ought to discourage Britt Larkin from any idea of moving back in. He'd have to cut the wire to do it, and our lookout in the shack would have a clear view and a good range of fire."

Ward Sullivan nodded as the wisdom of the scheme struck him. "Sounds good!" he agreed. "And cheap at the price. I'll send George down to Apache for a spool as soon as this buckboard is reassembled. Also staples and an extra hammer. It'll be the equal of a dozen guns for holding Larkin off Dragoon!"

The rancher seemed in good spirits this morning—the best mood Kincaid had seen on him since his coming. He knew that the accomplishments of yesterday had greatly heartened the man; he was grateful to have been responsible for Sullivan's renewed hope after the dark uncertainties of the recent past.

Apparently, whenever Ward Sullivan's confidence took a better turn he found expression for it in his attitude toward the black stallion. He walked over to the corral now, placed both hand on one of its poles, and drew a long breath into his lungs. An admiring gleam of possession was in his eyes as he murmured softly, lovingly, "You handsome devil!"

"Looks good this morning," Kincaid remarked; but his glance was on the man and not the horse.

"Oh, he's in fine shape. And we're better friends all the time. Why, he'll be eating out of my hand next thing you know. Just look!"

Sullivan fished up a cube of hard sugar and offered it through the bars. "Come on, boy! It's all right. Come on over and help yourself to something good!"

Diablo looked at the outstretched hand with a rolling, white-eyed stare; he dug a shoeless hoof into the corrals hard dirt, eased a little nearer, with Sullivan talking to him all the while. Still safely distant from the hand, he halted and put his neck forward, lips writhing back from ugly teeth; then, just short of touching the sugar, he shook out his mane violently and went skittering away to the far side of the pen.

The rancher gave it up, but he showed little disappointment. "You saw that?" he cried. "By jingo, he almost took it that time!"

"Yeah." Kincaid saw George looking in his direction and he winked. To his surprise, the man's sour face softened almost into the beginnings of a smile, and he returned the wink briefly. It was the first contact Kincaid had yet made with the strange and silent cowhand.

Still grinning a little, he left them and walked over to the house, thinking of breakfast. But as he stepped up to the open door the grin faded. Recollection of what had occurred here the evening before turned him sober and ill at ease as he reached for the knob of the screen.

He heard, within, a quick tapping of heels and then the sound of a door being slammed, hard; and when he crossed the threshold he found the kitchen empty. Yonder, the closed door of Claire Sullivan's bedroom told where she had gone. She was serving notice that she refused to stay in the same room alone with him.

Jaw muscles bunching, Kincaid let the screen jangle behind him and deliberately crossed the puncheon floor, a spur trailing. The coffeepot on the back of the stove was warm to his hard and calloused palm; he opened the cupboard, rummaged for a china cup, and, filling it from the big earthenware pot, had his meager breakfast standing. The warmed-over brew tasted bitter to him, but he took his time. He emptied the cup twice, placed it on the pine-plank drainboard.

"All right," he told the closed door then. "You can have your kitchen back now. I'm finished."

Rolling a smoke, he left the kitchen without hurry. But he could not feel as coolly indifferent about this as he would have liked to pretend. . . .

George's wire-purchasing trip to town in the buckboard would use up what was left of the morning. Kincaid gave him orders to bring the wire out to Dragoon Meadow as soon as he got back with it; then, with an ax and an old set of posthole diggers lashed to his saddle strings, he headed for there himself, meaning to get the mesquite posts cut and set and ready for the wire when it came.

On the way he picked up Macready, back from inspecting a seep spring that had shown signs of drying up as summer deepened its hold upon the range. Having spent the night in the Dragoon cabin with Rooster, Mac knew nothing yet of the jaunt Kincaid and Sullivan had taken down below or of their brush with the Mayes riders. Jingling toward Dragoon, Kincaid told him the story and heard his dry comment.

"We've done a lot," the old puncher observed, "in the less than two days you been here! We've brought them range-grabbing skunks to a dead halt, and now we're crowding back a little. Just wait'll Britt Larkin sees four strand of bob wire holding him off Dragoon, for good!"

Ross Kincaid didn't contradict him. It was, indeed, a very decent showing. If he could keep up the pressure, Sullivan's enemies might be pushed into some reckless move that could be used to trap them.

At the camp they found Rooster Adams strangely silent and looking a little white around the mouth. Mac, disturbed, tried to find out if anything was wrong but could get nothing out of him. Kincaid decided whatever might be the matter it was the youngster's own business, and he had best be left alone with it. So he called Macready off him and proceeded to lay out the job of fence building.

As he had suggested, a line of wire well anchored at either wing of the gap would effectively close the Meadow to Larkin beef—unless Britt wanted to brave the gunfire of Block S men forted within the shack. Kincaid measured off the distance to be spanned, figured the number of posts he would require. Then, as Rooster went to work with the post-hole digger at the points Kincaid had marked out for him, the other two mounted and headed for a mesquite thicket.

Kincaid used the ax, stripped to his waist and enjoying the sweat and the free working of his strong back muscles: clean, exhausting physical labor such as this was something in which he did not often have the chance to indulge. As the posts were ready, old Mac put a saddle rope on them and snaked them over to the fence line.

So they worked like that through the middle of the day, spelling each other; and by the time George pulled in with a gleaming new spool of wire bouncing heavily in the rear of the buckboard, the holes were dug and the post set up, ready.

There was news in Apache. George related it in his laconic way: John Dalhart, patrolling the breaks last night, had stumbled across cattle thieves trying to make off with a jag of his steers and had given them a running chase. This morning, checking again by daylight, he'd found one of the rustlers dead and had identified him as a Star rider named Blondy Hill.

Mac heard the information with a broad, yellow-toothed grin. "So they found him, did they! Well, now, let's watch old Charlie Mayes wriggle out of this one!"

As a matter of fact, though, the Star owner had already been called in and questioned. Seemed he'd told Dalhart and the sheriff that Hill was no responsibility of his. He'd discovered the man was a border jumper and fired him off the ranch not two days previously.

Macready's grin faded. "My Gawd! You mean the sheriff swallered that?"

Kincaid broke in: "Why not? His mind's already made up on this rustling; to have to think about suspecting somebody else now would only mess up his preconceived ideas. Just the same," he added, "let Charlie Mayes make one more misstep, and this business of Blondy Hill will be remembered, all right. He'll hardly talk his way out a second time."

"Yeah," grunted Mac. "If he's got sense to know when to be scared, I'll wager Charlie's shakin' in his boots. Or if he ain't he should be. . . ."

A bait of grub in the line shack; then, at Kincaid's order of "Well, boys, let's string some wire!" the four of them went out to finish the job. A wheel of the buckboard made a handy wire stretcher. They put the line up tight and solid. They did not put in any gate.

Afterward Macready set a tin can atop one of the posts, and Rooster, in the cabin doorway, sent it spinning with a single bullet from his saddle gun. Grinning, Mac retrieved the punctured can and put it in place again. "There!" he grunted. "Anybody comes monkeying around this, a shot at that can should be enough to warn him off. If not, the second one will teach him his mistakes—for good!"

The day was nearing a close. They piled their tools into the buckboard, and George and Mac headed with it toward the ranch. Macready would be back in a couple of hours to join the Rooster in his nightly vigil. Kincaid didn't go along. In answer to their questions he said merely, "I got a little riding to do. I'll be in later on." He picked up a few odds and ends of grub from the shack, to make his evening meal of in the saddle, and rode out alone.

Looking back once, he saw the new fence as a golden streak of reflected sunset, shimmering at the mouth of the gap. Rooster Adams was toting an armload of stovewood into the shack. Frowning a little, Kincaid reflected again, I wish I knew what was eating on him! But there was no answer to this, and he dismissed it.

He touched up the grulla with the spur, sending it northward through the lengthening shadows that laced these hills. Northward, toward Star. . . .

X   GOOD MAN—BAD HORSE

For two hours and longer, while night settled across this parched land and blotted out its rugged contours, Kincaid squatted in the concealment of a brushy slope above Star headquarters and watched and listened to what went on below. Chain smoking, shielding the glow with his palm, he laid a scatter of quirly butts around him. He heard the raucous life of Charlie Mayes' crew in their home quarters, heard harsh voices raised in sudden anger, then as quickly booming into laughter. He wasn't near enough to distinguish more than an occasional loud obscenity, but eavesdropping was not his purpose.

If any of Mayes' crewmen meant to do more night riding this evening, he intended to know it and to follow when they left the ranch . . . a much simpler matter, certainly, than trying to pick up sign down on the flats, as he had learned through his experience the night before.

Time dragged out, however, and no one rode away from

headquarters. A man came from the house once to check on the horses in the night corral, then went inside again. And presently Ross Kincaid left his perch and stole unobtrusively to where the grulla waited. He caught up the cinches, swung astride, and eased away into the starry darkness.

So Charlie Mayes was staying close to home this evening —scared, no doubt, by the mishap last night and the death of Blondy Hill. But what about Britt Larkin? Though they worked together, they didn't necessarily co-ordinate their night-riding activities. He toyed with the thought of drifting over toward Leaning 7 and having a look at developments there, then decided against it.

Larkin's men would be gone by this time if they were riding. There could be no gain and a good deal of risk in trying to get as close to the Leaning 7 buildings as he had managed here at Star. He decided finally to return to the Dragoon line shack instead.

He realized that he was very tired. He had pushed hard since he came here, with little chance of recuperating from the long ride down to this border graze. And today the unaccustomed labor with ax and posthole digger had fatigued him more than he knew. Muscles of back and shoulders felt painfully stretched and stiff. He figured he had earned at least one full night's sleep.

Still, it was close to midnight when he rode in on the line shack at Dragoon Meadow. Starlight glinted on the glass in the shack's window, outlined the corral behind it. There was something wrong, instinct told him suddenly; and then reason made it clear. Only a single horse was in the pen, and he could see no other mount running anywhere on the flat. There should have been two. . . .

He reined in and listened a moment before lifting his leg tiredly across and stepping down from leather. In the doorway he paused again, hearing the heavy breathing of a man asleep. He got a match and raked it across the doorjamb, and as it leaped to light he scanned the interior and found Rooster Adams, alone, stretched out in one of the bunks.

Kincaid spoke the boy's name.

But Rooster was a sound sleeper, and, throwing aside the burnt-down match, he groped his way across the room, guided by the snoring. There should be a lamp somewhere, but he didn't know where to locate it. Instead, he dug another sulphur stick from his shirt pocket, and as he leaned to shake Rooster awake he snapped the second match upon his thumbnail.

Rooster came slowly out of it; he mumbled something under the prod of Kincaid's hand upon his shoulder, and his eyes wavered open, drugged with sleep. They reflected in twin points of brightness the light of the match Kincaid was holding in front of him.

Then all at once the boy's eyes shot wide, and out of a mouth contorted by sudden terror a shriek burst from him. After that he was fighting Kincaid, almost as though trying to escape from the flame on which his staring eyes were pinned. Startled, Kincaid backed off, and the sulphur dropped from his hand, guttered out, and plunged the room again into darkness that rang with the echoes of the boy's frightened scream. At once Rooster subsided, but Kincaid could hear him panting, sobbing with fear.

"What the hell's the matter with you?" he snapped.

The sobs choked off. Rooster's voice, strained and unnatural, said, "Kincaid?"

"It's me. You really woke up fighting. Have a bad dream or something?"

Again a silence, and then the boy said huskily, "Yeah—yeah, I guess that was it. A bad dream. I have 'em, sometimes."

Obscurely, Kincaid felt dissatisfied with this explanation. "You sure that's all it was?" he demanded, but got no answer from the darkness. And he was too tired and too much concerned with other matters to press this one further.

He said, "Where's Macready?"

"I . . . dunno." Rooster's voice was steadier now, the first hysterical tremor gone from it. "He never showed up tonight. I know he expected to. I've been wondering if something could be wrong at the ranch?"

Kincaid considered, standing there in the pitch-black

room. He pulled off his hat, ran a hand through sweat-sticky hair. He didn't want to ride further tonight, but a nagging doubt had crept into his thoughts and this would goad him now and keep him from rest until he knew for sure. He sighed, dragged the hat on again.

"I'll go in and see what's up," he said heavily. "I'm leaving the grulla and switching my hull onto your bronc."

"All right. I hope it ain't anything."

At the door Kincaid turned to add, "Don't have any more nightmares, kid!" But he got no answer.

Wearily, he hauled the saddle off his gelding and gave the animal a slap, turning it loose to find grass and water and roll the saddle soreness from its body. He brought Rooster's pinto out of the corral, cinched on the gear, and hauled himself up again into leather. He had not even been out of it long enough for it to cool.

He pointed toward the ranch, and the fresh mount leaped forward under him to the bit of the steel.

. . . Light glowed at every window of the little house and bunk shack, and at that late hour it told Kincaid beyond any doubt that something was indeed wrong. He dug a final spurt of speed out of the roan and approached at a hard run; and as he bore in upon the yard he saw George come slouching out of the bunk shack. He hauled to a dust-spurting stop and leaned from saddle to demand harshly, "What's going on?"

The silent one merely jerked his head toward the house, but his face was dark with emotion. Kincaid, knowing he could get nothing more out of him, tossed the man his reins and swung down, moved stiff-legged toward the house.

Macready came through the door as Kincaid approached. The latter demanded harshly, "Well?"

"It's Sullivan," the old man answered, and moved aside to let him enter. On the threshold Kincaid paused.

Across the shabby kitchen another door stood open; and there, in the golden glow of lighted candles, he saw the blocky face of Ward Sullivan. Eyes closed, fully dressed, Sullivan lay stretched out full length upon the bed; his hands were crossed upon his breast.

Dully, uncomprehending, Ross Kincaid reached up and fumbled off his sweat-stiffened sodbuster. He tossed it at the table, not caring that it struck the edge and dropped to the floor instead. Then on leaden legs he crossed the kitchen and went through to stand beside the bed, gazing with dazed emotion at the kindly face, stilled now in death; and at the strong hands with a crucifix placed beneath their crossed palms.

"How did it happen?" he demanded. "Who——?"

"Diablo," said Mac behind him.

Kincaid turned, scowling at the old man in puzzled lack of understanding.

"The horse," Macready explained impatiently. "The black. This afternoon Ward said he was going to ride him. Diablo threw him off against the fence and then stomped him before we could get into the corral. . . ."

The bitter irony of this struck Kincaid with staggering force. With the tide setting at last in Ward Sullivan's favor —to have this! His life snuffed out; and not, as might perhaps have been expected, by a bullet from his enemies, but in an utterly irrelevant and meaningless kind of death. . . .

Then from the doorway Claire Sullivan spoke in a bitter, dead tone: "You killed him. You killed my father, Kincaid!"

They faced her. Macready exclaimed hoarsely, "Don't talk nonsense, girl! You know he had nothin' to do with it!"

"He killed him," she repeated, but her eyes that rested on Kincaid were as dead as her voice, the fires of hatred burned out in them and leaving only the cold ashes of tired despair. "He came here and filled Ward Sullivan with false hope and confidence. And it was that sent my father out there into the corral thinking he could ride that monster. He would never have tried it before."

Her unreason and twisted logic held Kincaid staring at her for a long and silent moment. He wanted to answer her but knew no use in it; she would not have listened and he felt no desire to quarrel with her now. Shock still showed in her face, which appeared haggard but softened by the glow of the candles by the bed and by the bright cascade of her hair which, unbraided, fell richly to the shoulders of the dressing gown she clutched about her.

Then without speaking to her Kincaid turned back to the old man. "Where's the bronc?"

"Still in the corral. Nobody's gone near him since it happened."

With fierce resolution Ross Kincaid swung out of that room, brushing past the girl in the doorway. He went through the kitchen, and with his hand on the screen door told Mac, across his shoulder, "Fetch a lantern." After that he went out into the darkness, boots crunching hard earth in long strides toward the breaking corral.

He was standing staring through the bars when Macready came running with a lantern swinging in his hand, scooting long shadows in pendulum strokes across the yard. Its gleam showed the black shape of the animal in the pen, shining on the sleek hide and the rolling eyes. Diablo, seemingly thrown into a kind of frenzy at sight of the men, was running wild in the confines of the corral, sniffing at the bars and then recoiling, hunting escape. The halter was still in place, one of the reins broken short where the horse must have stepped on it and snapped it off; he had managed to throw his saddle, and this lay in the dust, smashed and battered. Diablo must have taken out his fury against it.

Gun metal whispered against leather; the long barrel of Kincaid's six-gun winked lantern light as he brought it out and laid its muzzle against the black shape of the killer horse. He thought he heard a beginning protest break from Macready as his thumb hooked the hammer spur back, but Mac let this end short, uncompleted.

Then on a new impulse Kincaid lowered the gun without firing. Instead he said, "Put my saddle on him!"

"What!"

"You heard me! If this black devil thinks he can't be broken, I guess I'll teach him differently. Get my saddle on him!"

"But the black's a demon! You didn't see him when Ward Sullivan tried to go up top. Ward was a damned

good horseman; but this murderin' chunk of midnight——"

Kincaid merely turned his back on the old man's pro-
tests. He saw the silent George watching from a little distance, and he ordered, "Lend Mac a hand here."

It was a full-sized job for two men, getting leather on
the black a second time. Dust rose, gilded by the lantern
glow, as George and Mac circled with their ropes, reaching
for the horse, only to have him whirl free and let their
loops slap the dirt. The curses of the men mingled with
Diablo's angry trumpetings. Ross Kincaid, waiting outside
the corral, laid his folded arms against a pole of the fence
and put his head down upon them, resting and summoning
his strength.

He was a fool, of course. He was already near exhaustion
and in no shape to tackle such a job, and yet a stubborn
resolve had been planted in him and no man could have
dissuaded him from the thing he was determined to do.

Then a sudden shout from Mac and a squeal of rage
from the black told him that they had at last got a rope on
Diablo. He slipped through the bars and himself hefted
the big stock saddle and threw it on the shining barrel. It
took both punchers to hold the animal quiet enough for
Kincaid to get the hull settled and cinched tight. Afterward he examined the halter and decided it would do.

Mac warned him, "One rein is snapped short."

"There's enough of it," he answered, gathering the straps
in his hand. "Be ready to stand clear. . . ."

Then his boot was in the stirrup, and he sprang cleanly
into the hull.

He had barely hit leather when Diablo exploded with a
ferocity that even dragged a yell from the silent George
as the two men leaped wildly for safety. Kincaid was given
no chance to settle himself in the leather. Suddenly he was
astride a lurching, lunging demon and fighting to get his
right foot into stirrup before Diablo could unseat him.

By luck he made it; but that was only the beginning, of
squealing fury and neck-popping, stiff-legged joltings that
shook the very earth. Kincaid had topped bad horses on

occasion, but most of them had been rocking chairs by contrast with this. There was a ferocity in Diablo, and a quickness that brought the punishment in such fast succession that a man could not think or hardly even breathe. After the ride began he had not a moment to prepare himself for the next shock. Dazed, he felt the blood start from his nostrils, absorbed the poundings that started where iron-hard hoofs rammed against corral dirt and that ended by exploding with hammer force at the base of his skull.

But a cold anger was in Kincaid and a determination that would not yield. He stuck there, and he not only took what Diablo gave him but goaded the black demon on with raking spur rowels. The horse responded with redoubled frenzy, yet somehow Kincaid stayed where he was—choking on dust, his senses blurred, and time something that he had forgotten.

Mac's yell warned him of his danger even as he saw the high pole fence hurtling toward him out of the shadows. Diablo was seeking to rid himself of this second rider as he had the first one. Hastily Kincaid yanked his boot free, got his leg out of danger. The maneuver was barely timed. Next instant Diablo struck the fence—a full, sidelong smash that ought to have stunned and dropped him and that nearly hurtled Kincaid clear. Yet the horse caught stride, and the man dropped back into the saddle.

Finding the rider still upon his back seemed too much for Diablo. With almost a human scream the black reached for his leg with bared and wicked teeth, and Kincaid kicked him in the jaw. Squealing, the brute flung himself toward the fence again; then, just short of smashing into the bars, he whirled and began to rear.

Mac screamed, "Look out! He's gonna go over with you —against the fence!"

Kincaid heard the warning dimly; he had already guessed the black's wild intention. Jaw set, he groped and found his holster and dragged out the gun. And with the barrel, he clubbed Diablo's heavy skull.

The horse dropped to all fours, breath gusting out of him. He stumbled, collected himself, and started to buck;

and Kincaid, past all patience, struck again. He thought the black was going to go down under him, but Diablo kept his feet.

He was stopped dead, however. He stood on trembling legs, with head hanging and the wind sobbing in his muzzle. As abruptly as that, the battle was over.

Trembling himself, Kincaid swung quickly to the earth and went to the head of the horse, caught Diablo by the cheek strap. "You devil!" he grunted. "Sullivan named you well! But he was too good a man himself to know that there's only one way to tame the black heart inside of you. . . ."

Macready was beside him then, almost stumbling over his own feet. He croaked hoarsely, "You got him to a stand!"

"But not the way I liked doing!" Kincaid looked at the gun still in his hand. "I never had to pistol whip a bronc before. But it's the only lesson this one could ever learn."

"You figure he's broke?"

"Tamed—not broken. There's devilment aplenty left inside him, but he'll be a little slow after this to let it out!"

"I'd say," breathed Macready, "that I never saw a ride like that one!"

Kincaid shrugged. "Strip the gear off him and leave him be." And he turned and moved away on legs so weak that the knees seemed to possess no stiffening, and it was a supreme effort of will to keep himself erect.

George came hurrying, obviously thinking he needed help; Kincaid waved the man aside. He sleeved the beard stubble on his jaw and smeared the trickle of blood that came from his nostrils. Tang of blood was in his mouth.

Only then he saw the girl. She stood holding the lantern, free hand clutching the dressing gown about her, hair blowing wild in the night wind. Kincaid went to her.

He said, "Well, you got you a saddle pony!"

"No." Claire Sullivan shook her head—her eyes on his bloody face, her mouth drawn down. The lantern threw strange hoods of shadow across both of them. "I don't want him. He should belong to the man who can ride him."

Kincaid looked at her. "All right," he said finally. "I can use an extra mount in my string. I'll take the black." He added heavily, "I guess you'll be wanting me to take him and ride off this ranch—now that the ranch belongs to you. But I'm dead beat. You'll have to wait until tomorrow."

Her expression did not change, but she said, "We'll talk about it—tomorrow. Maybe I'll need you. Maybe I'll have to ask you to stay."

"That's up to you." Yet it was, he knew, a large and desperate admission on her part, and he thought about it as he turned and moved with uncertain steps toward the bunkhouse.

To have her father snatched away from her in the middle of the fight, and the whole weight of it shifted suddenly to her own shoulders, must have been a very great shock; it had shown her needs that transcended her own personal dislike of this man Ward Sullivan had brought in to help him in the same situation.

Kincaid struck the doorjamb with his shoulder, stumbling drunkenly. He reached his bunk and stood a moment, swaying and staring down at it. He knew he was a bloody mess and that he should try to clean himself up. Instead he let his battered body collapse to sprawl face downward upon the blankets and immediately was lost in the bitter sleep of exhaustion. . . .

XI   SMASH OF FISTS

They laid Ward Sullivan away in the little burial ground at the mission. They covered his body with a tarpaulin and placed it in the old buckboard, and every person on Block S went down to the town with it—Rooster Adams handling the team, Claire sitting stiffly beside him with a black shawl drawn over her fair hair, her eyes, unseeing, on the work-reddened hands folded in her lap. Macready and George held their horses at either side of the rig, where they could make sure the tarp-wrapped body weathered the rough jolting down from the bench.

Ross Kincaid, mounted on Diablo, left the others and went on ahead to Apache to make certain arrangements before the buckboard arrived. The black, once defeated, gave him little trouble. He took well to the saddle already, but he would allow no other man near him.

He seemed to have learned a certain respect for this tall rider who had tamed his wildness and brought him to a stand, and Kincaid managed him with an iron hand, offering him no chance to forget the lesson learned in the dust of the corral that wicked night.

In town Kincaid sought out an old Mexican cabinet-maker who kept a supply of coffins on hand, and from his own pocket paid for the finest one in stock—a simple pine box with a lining and with handles of beaten native silver. He had this delivered to the little mission and there held brief consultation with the priest. And when the buckboard with its grim burden arrived, the coffin was set up before the alter, ready.

At first Claire Sullivan refused to accept what he had done. Desperately poor herself, she wanted no charity from Kincaid; but he told her flatly, "I did this for Ward —not you. He paid me a month's wages, and I only worked for him a couple of days. This is the way I choose to return what I owe him. . . ."

So Ward Sullivan's body was transferred to the pine box, and Claire was left alone with him. From the open doorway Kincaid looked into the gloom of the building and saw her light a candle and then kneel before the crudely fashioned crucifix above the altar—a silent shape of grief, her black mantilla blending with the shadows.

The Mexican priest came out to him, hands folded within his voluminous sleeves and rope-soled sandals whispering. "You do not pray, then?" he murmured, his black eyes kindly and without censure.

Kincaid shook his head. "You'll have to excuse me, Father."

"Your heart is hardened," said Gregorio. "Or perhaps . . . I know what pride there is in you Americanos. It could

be the color of my skin that bothers you. You don't com-
prehend, as she does," he added, inclining his tonsured
head toward the girl before the alter, "that I am but the
instrument—the vessel. . . ."

"Get this straight," said Kincaid harshly. "Race has
nothing to do with it. I think you're a fine man, and if it
suits Claire Sullivan to have you bury her father, then I
certainly got no objections. My choosing not to pray is
another matter entirely. I respected Ward Sullivan too
much when he was alive to console myself with myths
now that he's dead and finished!"

"Finished," echoed the priest softly. "You're very sure
of that?"

"When I see a miracle—when I see a dead man walk—
then maybe I'll believe. Not until then." He fished a coin
from his pocket and tossed it into a sacrificial box inside
the door. "Go ahead and burn Sullivan a candle, for me.
I'm glad to help the church by paying for it. But don't try
to make me think that Ward Sullivan's dead eyes will see
its light, or any other. . . ."

It would be an hour until the burying itself. Kincaid
crossed the plaza to the sprawling hotel building, entered
the bar, and found himself the only customer. He ordered
a beer and let it stand, leaning his elbows upon the zinc
bar top while he had his thoughts about the solemn moment ahead of him.

Death was no stranger to him; more than one man had
been started on the cold journey to the grave by the gun
in Kincaid's holster. But a stranger's finish, or that of any
man that he had killed, could hold little emotion for him—
nothing akin to what he felt now at the passing of such a
one as Sullivan. By Kincaid's lights, there were few enough
really good men in the world that it could ill afford the loss
of any of them.

There was a wasteful indifference in the way life seemed
ready to discard its worthiest forms. And this thought confirmed Kincaid in his own hard core of cynicism. . . .

He looked up as a new man entered the room from the
lobby entrance. It was John Dalhart. Kincaid had seen him
earlier on the plaza, less than an hour ago, when the buck-

board bringing the Sullivan girl and her father's body rolled slowly up to the mission. He had seen how the rancher bared his fine white head respectfully, bowing slightly, as the rig came past him. Something in this recollection emboldened Kincaid now.

"Will you drink with me?" he invited as the bartender stepped up.

Dalhart considered him for a long moment with a level stare of sharp blue eyes. Then his broad shoulders lifted briefly within the tailored sack coat. He said in his broad southern voice, "I got no call not to, I reckon."

Kincaid nodded to the bartender and carried his beer along the counter to join the other man. Dalhart gave his order, and Kincaid rang a coin on the bar in payment, received a brief nod above the rim of the glass before the old rancher drained off his drink.

"Maybe," said Kincaid slowly, studying this man above his own half-drained glass, "you'd pay me back with a little favor—one that wouldn't use up much of your time."

The blue eyes took on a careful, guarded look. "Which would be . . . ?"

"Come to the buryin'."

Dalhart set down the empty shot glass. There was a scowl now on his strong, patrician features. "You're trying to drag me into something."

"Only for the girl. There'll be few enough there; it would make her feel better if you came."

"Is that all the reason?" Cold suspicion rimmed Dalhart's words.

"No," Kincaid admitted. "Not quite all. I peg you for a fair man, Dalhart—and a gentleman. I know the opinion you had of Ward Sullivan; but whatever you believed about him, I figure it would run against the grain for you to hold any grudge against his daughter."

"If I go to Sullivan's funeral," said Dalhart flatly, "it means I'm putting my support behind Block S."

"Not at all. It merely shows decent respect for a neighbor's passing—and that you have no hostility toward the girl. Surely there's no cause to think wrong of Claire Sullivan, despite what was said about her father. Surely you're gentleman enough to do this much in helping her make a start as the new owner of her father's ranch—when God knows she has a tough enough time ahead of her!"

"Well," the other conceded, "it's true I don't wish her any hurt. I scarcely know the woman—can't say that she's left the ranch more than a half dozen times since they came to this country; and as you say, she's only a girl, whatever Sullivan himself might have been or done. Still," his tone hardened, "she's running the same crew. It's the same outfit, whoever's at the head of it!"

Ross Kincaid let his stare turn flinty. "Do they honestly look like an owl-hoot crew to you, Dalhart. Old Mac, and George, and—him?" He poked a thumb toward the door; across the sun-smitten plaza the bony frame of Rooster Adams leaned against a pole roof support, engrossed with boyish concentration in the task of rolling a cigarette.

Dalhart did not even bother to look where Kincaid pointed. He said, "It wasn't those I meant. . . ."

"I see. Me, then?"

"Exactly! Until you came I tried to keep an open mind on the talk about Sullivan, even though I've lost as heavily to the border jumpers as any owner in Apache. There was never any proof against him except his record—and any man can make a first mistake. I first began to have really serious doubts of him the day I learned who he had brought in here to be his foreman. I still have those doubts."

Kincaid's hand tightened on the ear of his beer mug, then went lax. He felt the sudden cramped hardness of bunched jaw muscles. "You're an old man," he said finally, "and a frank-spoken one too. So I guess I'll have to take that and swallow it.

"But it happens you're dead wrong. I admit I've worked for an outfit, on occasion, that wasn't above shady doings; but I tried to earn my own pay fairly. I have never put any man's brand on beef that didn't belong to him, however much he paid me. That's the truth."

"Reputation says otherwise," Dalhart answered unwaveringly. "If a man gets that kind of a name for himself, how am I to disbelieve it?"

The other considered and then, realizing he had no

answer, lifted the point of a shoulder in defeat. "All right," he admitted. "I guess I had that coming. Go ahead then and believe what you like about me—but don't condemn the girl. Not yet. And if she asks me to stay in the driver's seat, then I warn you that I intend staying.

"I don't like to drop a fight once it's started—and I wouldn't feel like much, riding away now and leaving her to the enemies that are out to break her."

John Dalhart inclined his silver-maned head, briefly. "I've made mistakes," he said, "and I'm not too small for apologizing when they're proved on me. But I've got to play the cards as I see them."

"Can't ask other than that, I suppose. And you won't come to the burying?"

"No. I've told you why I can't. I'm sorry."

"So am I—for Claire." Kincaid finished his mug, shoved it across the metal bar top. And with a final, curt nod he moved past Dalhart and through the lobby doorway.

For Rooster Adams, death was still an unfamiliar experience, and the passing of one who meant as much to him as Ward Sullivan had been a profound shock that shook his world to the core. Thought of Sullivan lying in that box before the altar and of what would be done to him in an hour—the lid shutting out forever the light of day, the earth mounding over him, closing him into the cold darkness—this had settled upon Rooster with a dispiriting weight from which he was not yet old enough to know that time would deliver him.

With the vague impulse to busy himself, and somehow rid his mind of the full burden of these thoughts, he had wandered into a store and bought a sack of makin's. Now he leaned in frowning concentration against a mesquite pole, under the shade of the store's tin arcade roofing, and practiced his inexpert hand at the difficult skill that old Macready had long since despaired of teaching him.

His bony fingers were fumbling and awkward; they could handle a hard rope but anything as small and insubstantial as a cigarette was beyond them. Rice paper twisted to shreds, and tobacco spilled into the dust, and with a grunt of disgust Rooster threw the ruined smoke away and tried another. The ground about his feet became littered with torn papers; the tobacco sack dangled by its string from his grim-set mouth as he worked patiently at this task.

A match head cracked; a voice at his elbow murmured, "Want a light, kid?"

Looking around, he saw Jack Beach grinning at him wickedly. And Jack shoved the flickering match into his face.

Rooster cried out in hoarse terror, tobacco sack falling from his mouth; his hand jerked and batted the match out of Beach's fingers. This excuse all he needed, the thick-shouldered man snarled something, and his fist swung, cracked hard against the side of the youngster's face.

The old mesquite pole bucked springily as Rooster's shoulders struck it; popped a warning. And then Beach, with a brutal joy of hurting, stepped against the Rooster and lifted his knee in a hard thrust.

Agony twisted through the lad and, with the other's mocking laughter grating in his ears, he doubled, caught at the wooden pole to save himself, and went pivoting around it to land on his knees in the dust. He heard Britt Larkin's foreman mouthing savagely, "Don't go knockin' things out of my hand, boy!"

Sobbing, Rooster tried to answer but could neither speak nor move, his muscles locked in cramping nausea . . . and suddenly heard a new voice, quiet but stinging with anger. Ross Kincaid said, "All right, Jack! You've been asking for this!"

. . . Beach had turned sharply, startled at this unexpected interruption. A flicker of fear ran across the muggy depths of his eyes, but it passed as he saw no gun in Kincaid's fingers; instead, Kincaid's hands were balled into fists. Confidence and real pleasure warped the other's blue-jowled face then, he being one who took keen delight in the challenge of hand-to-hand. His massive shoulders—misshapen in proportion to the rest of his saddle-whipped frame—rolled forward. The fist that had struck Rooster shot out in a sharp punch aimed at Kincaid's head.

But Kincaid was expecting this and managed to get his elbow up fast, blocking the punch. Then with Beach still off balance he sent his own right over.

It grazed the man's jaw, struck the heavy-plated muscle of his thick shoulder, and slammed him against the same post from which Beach's first wallop had sent Rooster reeling. This time the pole popped even louder, and a long crack formed down the length of the silvered, weathered wood. Dust sifted from the jarred roof overhead.

Rooster Adams had got a palm against the earth and was trying to shove himself upward. His face was white and twisted with agony as he cried hoarsely, "Damn it, Kincaid! He's my meat. . . ."

Unheeding, Kincaid sank a left jab into the foreman's body, just in under the short ribs. Wind tore from Beach's parted lips, but the blow stopped him for a second only. Then he was pushing away from the pole, and his big fists were flailing with the weight of those heavy shoulders behind them.

At the corner of the plaza the mountainous shape of Sheriff Griswold had appeared; he saw what was going on and broke into a dogtrot, his sagging flesh jouncing as he came along the pathway. And the fight went ahead unmindful of him.

Jack Beach had rocked Kincaid badly with one of his driving fists and was wading in to press this advantage. Indeed, he forced Kincaid to yield ground; he had the greater experience at this type of battle, and such training could not help but tell. But there was the high spur of indignation to drive Kincaid.

He knew he could end this at any moment he cared to shift his attack and go after the gun in his holster, but he wanted to punish Beach with the man's own cruel weapons —with the bruising smash of fists.

His heel struck a pool of powder-dry dust and twisted, slipping in the treacherous stuff. It threw him completely off stride, starting down to one knee, and at this a cry of satisfaction broke from Beach and he rushed forward. Kincaid knew the man would not hesitate to use his boot on an opponent momentarily unable to defend himself.

It was a bad moment, and he did the only thing he could: he threw himself prone under the swing of the foot that Jack Beach brought reaching for his head. Beach stumbled, nearly sprawling across Kincaid. Then, rolling in the choking dust, Kincaid had got free and was coming up.

His opponent's back was toward him, and Kincaid grabbed him by a shoulder, hauled him around, and slammed a fist into the middle of his face. He felt the sharp edge of a tooth against a knuckle, saw Beach stumble away with blood spurting from his mouth. But before he could move in to follow up the attack a ponderous figure edged into his path, and Port Griswold's rumbling voice was saying, "Let's stop this—right here!"

Kincaid caught himself and turned to face the sheriff. He was breathing hard, sweat and dust and blood on him. Yonder, Beach stood with his back against a building front, his head thrust forward and glaring at Kincaid. He cried hoarsely, "Jail him, Port! Or get out of the way and give me a chance to finish him. The guy picked a fight for no cause!"

"He's a liar!" Kincaid retorted. "He was roughing the kid."

The sheriff appeared to consider. He turned and put his slow, mastiff stare upon Rooster Adams, who stood with one hand clutching the cracked post for support and with a pallid, sick look on him. "What have you got to say about this?" he demanded.

"Nothin'!" retorted the boy. "Nothin' at all. I never asked for nobody fighting my fights for me."

Griswold looked at him a long, slow minute. And the sheriff had the look of one who smells something bad to which he cannot quite put a name.

As it happened, he was thinking of another morning, in the line cabin at Dragoon Meadow. There had been the same sickness in Rooster Adams' face, and the boy's refusal to make a charge or answer a direct question. There was even Jack Beach, who, he remembered, had had something to do with that other time. It all seemed a very strange coincidence, and the slow-witted sheriff knew only that he didn't like it.

He lifted his shoulders ponderously. "We'll let it drop. But I don't want it taken up again—not here, anyway. If you got a squabble that has to be settled, do it in private . . . understand?" There was a long-barreled six-shooter in Griswold's massive fist, and he motioned with it as he nudged Jack Beach on the shoulder. "Break it up, Jack! Drift!"

The foreman's mouth twisted; he ran a palm across his lips, looked at the blood, and then his muddy eyes went to Kincaid's face and to the boy's and back again to Kincaid. He said gruffly, "The hell with it!"

Turning to the sheriff then, he added, "Just don't think you're givin' me orders, Port! Britt wouldn't like that any. The tin badge you wear don't give you no leg to start acting high and mighty toward Leaning 7!"

Griswold didn't answer, though the threat must have dug deep. He stood and watched Jack Beach hitch his jeans and then swing off at a long stride through the shadow-and-sun strips of the arcaded store fronts. Afterward he told Kincaid, "It's a fact, Britt's gonna want to know why I didn't jail you on Jack's direct charge. Maybe I got my reasons; and I'll take care of Britt. But for Lord's sake, go easy in this town, mister!"

Ross Kincaid had leaned and got his sodbuster from the place where it had fallen. He beat dry dust out of it against a leg as he studied the sheriff, reading something here he hadn't suspected before. There just might be in Port Griswold a man worth reckoning with.

He said, "That's fair enough, Sheriff. Just as long as Britt Larkin's tough range boss leaves my crew alone, I'm glad to keep the peace." He turned to Rooster. "Come on, kid, over to the hotel and let's clean ourselves up. They'll be waiting for us at the mission not many minutes from now. . . ."

Rooster surlily offered him first turn at the wash basin, but Kincaid refused, preferring to wait with shoulders leaning against the hotel's rough rear wall as he watched the young-ster dab water on his face, wincing to the sting of the cut cheek. Neither spoke until the boy had nearly finished; then Kincaid asked, "Well, kid? You want to tell me about it?"

Face buried in the rough towel, Rooster Adams froze for an instant. Slowly then he lifted a cold, hostile stare to meet Kincaid's eyes. "About what?"

"You'd know better than I would," replied the older man with a shrug; but his tone was not unkindly. "Some-thing's been eating you these last few days . . . got you act-ing mighty funny. Now I'm beginning to think maybe it has something to do with Jack Beach. And I figure it's time you got it off your chest."

Rooster's mouth worked. His hands clenched on the coarse material of the towel . . . savagely flung it from him. "You're dreamin'! I got nothin' to bother me!"

"I think different."

"Well, you're wrong!" Rooster jerked his glance away, swung to pick his hat and jacket from the bench. Back turned to Kincaid, avoiding the older man's eyes, he began rolling down his sleeve with angry movements. "Anyway, a man has a right to his own private business without no one pryin' into it. That is, supposin' it was so."

Mildly Kincaid agreed with him. "Of course he does. Hell, it's nothin' to me, kid! Not unless it concerned Block S . . . and even that'll be none of my business now, I reckon."

The boy stabbed him a quick look. "You're goin' from here?"

"Unless Miss Claire says differently—and she's appar-ently not made up her mind. Ward Sullivan hired me; when Ward is in the ground, my connections here are at an end."

Rooster looked sober and troubled getting slowly into his jacket. Kincaid pushed away from the wall, picked up the tin basin to throw out the dirty water and run in fresh from the hotel pump. No more was said by either of them about what had been troubling the kid.

. . . The burying itself took but little time. A few words of Latin . . . Father Gregorio crumbling a clod of earth above the solemn box: there was little more ceremony than this. Ross Kincaid stood with Claire Sullivan. Old Macready's balding skull bowed to the fierce sunlight at her other side. There was George, and Rooster showing the effort of keeping back the unmanly tears that stung his eyes. There was no one else at all.

Afterward Kincaid took the spade and threw a shovelful of dirt upon the box, then ceremoniously passed the tool on to Mac and each of the others. With that, the thing was finished. Silently they turned away, leaving the rest of the job to the priest and a couple of Mexican gravediggers, who were leaning on their shovels a little distance away waiting to fill in the hole they had made.

Claire stumbled once or twice on the rough earth, as though blind to where she stepped, and Kincaid saw old Mac slip a hand under her arm to steady her. That was the only comforting gesture she received.

They had nothing more to delay them here, and the group left town a scant ten minutes later. The heat of the high sun was increasingly oppressive. Claire seemed uncomfortable so far away from the barren ranch, and so Rooster Adams gave vent to his own feelings by lashing up the buckboard horses. The riders kept pace, and they went along the road that way at a hard clip, the buckboard jouncing and a billow of dust churning up from hoofs and rolling wheels.

It was nearing the ford of Apache Creek, the hills lifting hard ahead, that they discovered a thing that made them come in on the place with a tightening apprehension.

Three riders were ahead of them. Their horses blocked the trail on the far side of the sun-bright water. One man sat slack in the saddle, knee hooked over the horn, while a second hunkered beside the stream and idly chucked stones into it. The third stood holding his horse's reins, slapping them against a palm. They looked as though they had stopped to water their mounts before crossing and, having sighted the approaching buckboard and the trio of horsemen grouped about it, were now waiting for them.

And the man in the saddle was Charlie Mayes; the other two, a pair of his tough bunkhouse crew. They were all wearing guns.

Macready said heavily, "We'll go right across. They wouldn't have the nerve to try and stop us. . . ."

As they slowed for the steep bank of the fording, the one who had been tossing stones into the water flung his last one and eased to a stand, lightly dusting his palms; the others remained just the way they were. The light rig struck the sharp, north-flowing current that ran swift and cold, this close to its source in the fishhook curve of the hills. The hoofs of the horses raised geysers of spray, slapping the shallow surface.

Then Kincaid saw that the buckboard team was lagging as they tackled the rise of the nearing bank, and he pushed Diablo forward. His hat came down in an arc against the off-bronc's flank, put it into the harness. Afterward he was going on—past the team and ahead of it—straight up the bank toward Charlie Mayes.

The latter sat and watched him come, unmoving, his white-stockinged sorrel directly blocking the trail. The scowl below his red mustache was dangerous; his eyes bored into Kincaid's. But at the last moment he gave the rein a jerk and, almost casually, pulled his mount out of the road. And the Block S outfit went by unhindered, without so much as a nod or a word from either group.

Kincaid was sure, however, that they had been only an inch away from an explosion. Probably audacity alone had avoided it. . . .

Then behind them Charlie Mayes called out: "Oh, Miss Sullivan!" and in a quick spurt of hoofbeats he roweled his sorrel after the buckboard. He was alone; his two men had remained behind at the ford. Looking back, Kincaid said sharply, "Hold it, Rooster! Might as well see what he wants."

Mayes came up at a canter, right hand lifted to hatbrim, left held high to show that it contained nothing but the reins. His whole manner was carefully unbelligerent. As his mount slid to a stop he raised his hat briefly to the girl and then settled it again on crisp, reddish hair. He said, "I been wanting to talk to you, ma'am. Now's as good a time as any."

"Is it?" said Claire without warmth. But she waited, and the restless horses stamped in the wet earth.

"A business matter," Mayes continued. "Of course there's no need my sayin' anything about your father's passin'—about how I regretted hearin' it. . . ."

"Reckon there ain't!" old Macready snapped, shifting in saddle with a look of sharp disgust on his weathered features. "No use wastin' our time with such talk!"

Mayes went ahead, ignoring this. "I'm wonderin'," he said, "about that property of yours—that ranch. Naturally, I suppose, you'll be thinkin' of selling and gettin' out from under, and as your neighbor I'd like to make you a bid on it. In fact, I'm prepared to give you my note right now— to be converted into cash at any time, on three days' notice."

Claire Sullivan heard him out without expression. "What makes you so sure I'm anxious to be rid of Block S?" she demanded then.

"Why, I took something of the sort for granted." He appeared a bit set back at any other possibility. "This is a hard country, miss; hard on the strongest of men. And naturally, you bein' a woman—and alone . . ."

"Only, I'm not alone, Mr. Mayes!"

The narrow face altered slightly; the reddish eyes flickered. Then Charlie Mayes let his mouth settle into a hard line, and his stare moved from the girl to touch each of her companions in turn. It came to rest finally on the face of Ross Kincaid.

"That's includin' you, Kincaid?"

The latter met his look, unyielding. "You're talking to the lady—not to me. I was hired by Ward Sullivan to rod the spread for him. Now there's a new owner. Her decisions, when she makes 'em, are what I'll be going by."

"Then I can only hope," said Mayes harshly, swinging his look again to the girl, "that you'll think real careful makin' 'em. If you'll forgive my sayin' it, your pa didn't put enough weight on what people thought of him, or he wouldn't gone around hiring professional killers like this Kincaid. I hate to see you blunderin' into the same mistake."

"It happens my decision is already made," Claire replied in a tone of stubbornness. "Ross Kincaid stays on the payroll—no matter who doesn't like it!"

The announcement had brought a sudden, stinging silence. Into this, Kincaid said quietly, "Thanks, Miss Claire. I'll do my best for you!" And he received a look from her that was different from any she had ever given him—that seemed, indeed, to hold real warmth.

The redhead's eyes had narrowed to points behind slanted lids. "I see," he clipped. "Well, I'm sorry. Mighty sorry indeed . . ."

And abruptly he had whirled his sorrel and was spurring away from there without a backward glance. The very set of him in the saddle told the pent-up rage that rode him. He didn't stop when he hit the ford but went across it, splashing water high, and at once his two crewmen had flung themselves into leather and were going after their chief, hard upon his heels.

Rooster Adams said sourly, "Well, that was tellin' him! That was givin' the dirty crook something to think about!"

"It gave me an idea or two myself," said Kincaid. "A personal call I want to make . . . You go ahead. I'll join you at the ranch later."

"Ridin' these hills alone?" old Macready muttered disapprovingly. "You do too much of that, Kincaid. Now, especially, you're a marked man. Ward was strong enough to stand by himself, but with you out of the way they might figure Claire would be willing to come to terms."

"I can take care of my hide," Kincaid retorted, brushing aside this argument.

He pulled back and waited until Rooster got the buckboard team in motion again, and still sat there looking thoughtfully after the rig and its outriders until they had gone from sight into the rocks and brush and tumbled brakes below the bench.

Claire's decision to retain him as foreman, he was thinking, probably was the only one she could have made in light of the pressures that were on her and the lack of any other help to which she might turn. What did surprise him was the look she had given him. It had been very nearly a friendly one—the first such he had ever had from her; and it made him wonder a little.

He was chewing these thoughts as he rode at an easy gait past the trail forking and the signpost there and turned Diablo into the left-hand branch that led to Leaning 7.

Little sign of activity showed around the ranch headquarters; the crew would be out on range chores most probably. A trickle of piñon smoke lazed from the chimney of the cook shack, melting against the brilliant sky and the winking heads of the cottonwoods. Kincaid rode in toward the house and there amid the bright splash of the flower beds saw the slim figure in white.

He had failed to notice her at first, so well did she blend with the dazzling whiteness of the fresh-painted adobe front of the house. The sound of his horse approaching made her aware of his presence at almost the same instant, and she straightened from her work, turning quickly with a pair of pruning shears in one hand.

Kincaid saw her eyes widen with alarm as her breast lifted to a sharp intake of breath. For himself, he was able only to reflect that any man—whatever opinion he might have of Irene Larkin—could in the first moment be struck simply by the animal handsomeness of her. She knew how a dress should be designed in order to enhance the full attractiveness of her figure. The one she wore now was much too expensive a garment for digging in a flower garden. Its white purity set off her coloring wonderfully, and he noticed that she wore long gloves to protect her arms from the grilling heat of the sun. The woven, broadbrimmed Mexican hat shielded the fair, exposed flesh of her throat.

She said quickly and breathily in a hurried whisper that scarcely reached to him where he had halted the black only a few feet away: "Be careful! He's here. . . ."

Kincaid had lifted a hand to touch his hatbrim. He dropped it again, frowning; but before he could speak the bulky shape of Britt Larkin emerged from the doorway of the house and moved out to the edge of the arcade shadow.

Larkin said, "Irene!" in a voice that held the barbed edge of a saw; as she turned he gave her a jerk of the head that summoned her to move from between himself and the visitor.

Then he and Kincaid were facing each other—the latter shifting over to a comfortable position in the saddle but with no move to dismount. Larkin, spreadlegged at the rim of the shadow, thumbs in belt, had his head lifted to squint at his visitor from under the gallery roof.

"Well!" grunted Larkin. "Somehow I didn't figure to see you again. Or maybe you come around to say good-by to—somebody."

Kincaid echoed him mildly. "Good-by? You mean you'd thought I'd be leaving?"

"Your boss is dead, ain't he?"

"But I don't like to quit any job half-finished. So I'm staying on."

Larkin took this in silence. That it was unpleasant news, he showed in his scowl and in the way he brought up his hand, ran the knuckle of the thumb across his misshapen nose; he was stalling, working out his thoughts.

He said, "Then maybe *that's* why you came around—to tell me so. Or—was it some other reason?" And his suspicious stare cut quickly to Irene, standing a little apart and watching them both; perhaps he thought to catch something revealing in her expression, but she showed him nothing.

"Another reason," agreed Kincaid. "A sense of fairness, maybe. The first night we met, Britt—down in Apache—you showed yourself a man who liked to run up a bid on something he wanted. I thought it would only be the neighborly thing to let you have your chance this time too."

"What the hell you talking about?" demanded Larkin. "Bid on what?"

"Block S. Your friend Charlie Mayes just came to Miss Sullivan with a cash offer."

"You lie!" The words were a sudden roar of stung fury. "He never done that!"

"Oh, but he did!" insisted Kincaid pleasantly. "She turned him down; still, I thought if you'd care to up his price . . ."

The rancher's face had changed color, a tide of angry red flowing slowly upward from his thick neck and across his craggy features. "Quit funnin' me!" he gritted. "I know damn well she won't sell, to me or Charlie either one—not with you around to keep her from it!"

Kincaid only grinned at him. He had worked his purpose here; the news of Charlie Mayes' offer, he knew, must have its effect on the big man—must drive one more small wedge into the split that already existed in their partnership. Having done as much, he was content to leave Larkin to chew this matter in private and suck what bitterness he could from it.

"All right," he said, and took the reins. "It was just a thought. I figured you'd like to hear the latest concerning property I know you've got your eye on. But I agree you're probably right. You'll never own Block S, Larkin—or any part of it!"

"That's to be seen," muttered Larkin, and lapsed into silence. He watched as Kincaid gave his wife a pleasant nod and a tip of hatbrim. But at the last minute, looking at the black horse that carried Kincaid's saddle, he blurted a question just as his visitor made as though to pull away.

"Hey! Ain't that the broomtail Sullivan choused out of the hills? The one that killed him?"

"It is, as a matter of fact. His daughter didn't want the nag, so I took him over."

"You don't seem to be having any trouble taming him."

Kincaid agreed and added with pointed significance, "But I'm pretty hard to kill, Britt. Some have found that out—and found it worth remembering. . . ."

Later, working northward alone across the hills onto Block S graze, Kincaid let his thoughts touch upon the woman, Irene. It was irony that he, who had small patience with women, should be caught here between two of them —a spoiled, ambitious creature like Irene Larkin on the one hand, and Claire Sullivan on the other with her chilled, reserved hostility and her potential good looks and femininity that had never been given their chance to bloom.

The physical attraction lay with the first; but for the second he was beginning to know a growing, grudging respect, born of the will and fortitude that she was showing now in the bleak aftermath of her father's death. But both of these women in their various ways promised him nothing but trouble. . . .

He came over a crest and into the head of a shallow, slanting ravine that fed downward into a sort of bowl of greasewood and boulder rubble. At his left hand a steep hill face, sparsely timbered with scattered scrub cedar, broke away abruptly to become a barren rock slant facing a nest of good-sized boulders on the lower ground just opposite. Between these boulders and this rock face Kincaid's route lay across the shallow bowl. A dead stillness rested upon the afternoon, except for the sluff of the black's shoeless hoofs coming down through the rubble of the ravine.

Then ahead and to his left Kincaid heard a slide and rattle of loose stone, and to his outdoorsman's instincts this was like a warning shout.

He pulled rein, his eyes searching. He caught the movement before it quite ended, saw the last ripple of loose stone hit the gravel tailings at the foot of that rock slant, and at once let his stare run quickly upward to the eroded lip thirty feet above. Nothing there to break the skyline— nothing to explain what had caused that brief gravel slide to start down the rock. Maybe a lizard breaking for its hole . . . But Ross Kincaid had not lived this long in a dangerous trade by accepting the first, easy explanation for troubling phenomena.

So he pulled the black sharply aside, pointing toward the scrub cedar. And on the instant, the first shot sprang up: a rifle, slapping sharply against the stillness. It came from the low boulders to the right of the trail and close enough that the powerful bullet went screaming past Kincaid with an audible sound. The black trumpeted, reared.

Kincaid˙ had started a movement for his holster gun, but he cursed and checked that, for his hands were suddenly too full with managing the horse to give him a chance to use a weapon.

Diablo, as yet still more than half-wild and only partially broken to the saddle, was utterly unfamiliar with gunfire. Kincaid realized now that he would be of no use at all in this ambush. There was no choice but to be quit of the horse as hastily as possible.

He set the spurs and sent Diablo buckjumping hard for the dark green of the cedars; and more bullets followed him.

XIII   THE SMELL OF FEAR

He made the trees untouched, burst into them, with Diablo's slick hoofs fighting the loose rubble and the slant. The growth of timber was sparse, making a thin screen; nevertheless, he dropped from the saddle and with the reins anchored Diablo to one of the stunted tree boles, having difficulty doing this because the animal was nearly wild with terror.

Kincaid got the knot secured, however, and then slipped his belt gun and stood a moment considering, one hand set against the rough bark of the tree. The shots had died now, and there was again silence, all the more complete for the remembered medley of the guns. How many there were he could not clearly guess—three, maybe more. He thought regretfully of his other mount—the grulla; that was a battle-wise animal that had carried him unflinchingly out of situations as bad as this or worse. But no, he had had to ride the half-wild Diablo, and now, as a result, the first break of danger had him pinned down afoot and partially helpless.

In these trees he could not get a clear view of the ground below him or the boulders, where he judged at least a couple of the gunmen must be staked out. But, turning upward, he could see the rim of the rock slant overhanging the trail and clearly made out the head and shoulders of a man as he moved slowly into view and poised there against the sky for a moment looking down.

The six-gun lifted in Kincaid's hand, then lowered. The silhouette had moved silently out of sight again. He had recognized it, however—knew he'd seen this man earlier standing beside his horse at the Apache Creek crossing. And this fact identified the rest of his attackers.

Charlie Mayes would not have had time to pick up further help for this ambush; so there were only the three of them. Mayes and the other tough hand must make up the pair hidden in the boulders below the trail.

Accordingly, Kincaid weighed and shaped a quick decision.

The scrub cedar cloaking this ridge, though sparse, grew heavier farther up. To reach that thicker growth he must cross a relatively barren stretch of steep, loose earth, exposed for a moment to the guns of his enemies, but it was a necessary risk. He picked his goal and, suddenly breaking loose from shelter, went toward it at a run, doubled over to make as small a target as possible as he quartered across the open slope.

Immediately they saw him, and immediately their bullets started reaching. He had gone less than a dozen steps before he knew he had chosen badly. The loose, sliding rubble caught at his boots, holding him back and making a target of him. Bullets began to kick up stinging clouds of dirt, pocking the slope about him as the riflemen quickly zeroed in. And though he twisted and dodged, he seemed unable to get free of the searching leaden fingers; they seemed to come at him from a dozen different directions, with uncanny skill at seeking him out.

A windfall lay across the slope, and he dived for this protection. As he threw himself prone, hugging the narrow shelter, he glimpsed one of the riflemen below him stand-

ing behind his boulder, where he had risen with saddle
gun at shoulder to throw off shot after shot. Kincaid lifted
to an elbow, threw his six-gun at arm's length across the
weathered log, and fired twice, hardly more than quick
snap shots. But one of them was good, and Charlie Mayes'
second tough flung his rifle away as he stumbled backward
and then broke and went down, arms and legs sprawling.

That left Mayes, himself, in the boulders and the other
man atop the steep ledge. And that one now flung a bullet
that clipped dead branch from the windfall only inches
from Kincaid's head as he flopped back. He realized the
log could give him no protection at all from that direction.

So he had to get out of there, and fast; and coming to
hands and knees, he started at a crawl along the upward
side of the slanting log, where Mayes at least could not
target him. The man on the rim continued his fire as fast as
he could work the lever, but with haste that was too great
for a moving target. Still unhurt, though slivers of bark
leaped within inches of his scrambling shape, Kincaid
reached the tangle of roots that held the fallen tree in place;
vaulting the log, he quickly put this between himself and
both his enemies.

He poked his gun through the rotted mat of roots and
fired once. He missed, but he at least sent the man on the
rim pulling hastily back from sight, which gave him the
moment he needed to turn and lunge the remaining yards
for decent cover.

Once in the thicker fringe of cedar growth he did not
stop but went on at a run, slipping and sliding and from
time to time stabbing a hand against the loose soil of the
slope or catching at a tree trunk to keep himself on his feet
in the treacherous footing. He had to work fast before they
guessed what he was up to. For the moment the guns had
fallen off, leaving a shocked silence in ears that had grown
accustomed to the sound of them. Kincaid thought he
heard the men calling back and forth, comparing notes
and debating; but the confused echoes made their words
unintelligible to him.

Then he had reached the head of the slope, and below
him the trees halted and barren rock spread out to the

sharp drop off. Directly on the rim, back turned toward Kincaid, Mayes' second killer squatted on his knees peering cautiously over, with one hand balancing himself and the other holding a six-gun. The man's rifle, muzzle smoking, lay beside him—shot dry, likely.

"He's in them trees, Charlie," he was calling now into the bowl. "You cover from down there. I'll swing wide and drive him out."

The answer came thinly to Kincaid; he heard only the tail end: ". . . damned careful about it!"

And then the man on the rim was scrambling about, starting to his feet . . . and he saw Kincaid.

His mouth gaped open; belatedly he thought of the gun in his hand and started to level it. And Kincaid fired with no more compunction than he would have felt in killing a deadly snake.

He did not aim for the body, however. His bullet struck just where he placed it, smashing into the man's gun arm and sending it flopping grotesquely while the weapon sprang from his hand unfired, and the man himself cried out and toppled sideward. The force of the lead striking came very near to throwing him over the edge of the rim to the ground thirty feet below. He lay where he fell, twisting and moaning; and Kincaid was hurrying quickly forward as the voice of Charlie Mayes shouted a startled question.

Reaching the one he had felled, Kincaid saw the dullness of shock beginning to fade from the hurt man's eyes and quickly knelt to clamp a hand across his mouth. He showed the fellow his smoking gun muzzle.

"Tell him it's all right," he ordered. "Call down. 'I got him.' Otherwise no doctor will ever have a chance to tie up that elbow!"

The eyes that stared at him above the silencing hand burned bright with hatred and thawing pain. Down in the bowl Charlie Mayes called a second time.

Kincaid touched gun muzzle to his prisoner's throat. "How about it?" he gritted.

A swallow ran convulsively through the unshaven throat, and he could feel it stir the barrel of the gun. When the head nodded, Kincaid removed his palm. With dry lips and a voice that had a wild strain in it his prisoner cried hoarsely: "Got—got him, Charlie...."

Immediately, as a precaution, Kincaid clapped his hand into place again and stayed like that a moment longer, listening to the hurt man's breathing and to the murmur of the cedars at his back. Below there was the scrape of boots sliding over rock. Coming to his feet then, Kincaid stepped to the edge of the rim, his gun slanting down into the bowl beneath.

"Drop the guns, Charlie!" he warned sharply. "Or I'll drop you on top of them!"

Directly below, full in the open into which that cry had tolled him out of his hiding place in the boulders, Charlie Mayes stood with head jerked upward. His lean shape was foreshortened from this elevation so that he seemed nothing more than head and shoulders with boots projecting somewhere beneath; but he made a good target, nonetheless, and Kincaid's sights were directly on him. Mayes had no chance and he knew it.

"Don't!" he bawled. "Don't shoot me!" With a convulsive gesture he flung the rifle that he carried, end over end; it clattered into the rocks. "You wouldn't murder a gent, Kincaid!"

"I dunno—wouldn't I? It's twice now you've tried doing it to me. Why should I let you go, maybe to notch my hide the next time?" But then before the other could stammer an hysterical answer, Kincaid added harshly, "Take off that six-gun and toss it after the rifle. And then start walking!"

Mayes, fumbling hastily at the shell-belt buckle, asked frantically, "Where?"

"Straight down the trail . . . to that chimney rock a hundred yards from here. I'll watch until I see you've reached it; and if you dare to move away from it or try any tricks while I'm getting my bronc—I'll kill you for sure! Now walk!"

Soon afterward, mounted once more on Diablo, Kincaid rode out of the little bowl that had nearly proved a murder trap for him and found Mayes waiting stolidly where he had been ordered. The lean fox face scowled blackly at him as he came up to the tall chimney rock. Not having been shot down in his tracks the instant his enemy managed to gain the advantage, Mayes had found time to regain a measure of confidence. He demanded now, "What do you think you're going to do with me?"

"I know what I'd like to do," Kincaid grunted. "But there's a man back there on the ledge with a smashed arm who'll bleed to death if he isn't got to a doctor . . . not to mention the other one in the rocks that may be dead already. On account of them—and for no other reason— I'm turning you loose. But don't make any mistake about it: You're finished!"

Charlie Mayes looked up at him from slanted eyes that gleamed with pure malevolence. His upper lip drew back. "You think so? The hell with you!"

"You hounded Ward Sullivan," the other continued, "and now that he's dead you've already started working on his daughter. Up to this your nasty crookedness has meant nothing at all to me personally—your border-running that you laid to Sullivan's blame; even the bullet you threw at me the night I first came to Apache. They were no more than the hazards that brought me good pay for the job I did.

"But Sullivan was a man, and he could fight back; now in trying your sneaking ambush you're hitting through me at Sullivan's girl. And it won't work, Charlie! This time you've gone too far!"

As the words slapped into him the rancher's face slowly lost its sneering arrogance. The hard warping of the mouth slackened; a kind of gray pallor crept into the narrow features. "Are—are you threatenin' me?"

"I'm just telling you facts, Charlie. I'll let you go, now, so that these men can be got to a doctor for whatever good he can still do them. But come sunup tomorrow, the range is closed to you! If you're still in this country, I'll come looking for you and I'll kill you—and all the gun hands in your bunkhouse won't save your stinking hide! And after that's done, I guess I may as well go after Britt Larkin, too, and finish this job while I'm at it!"

He was not merely talking. There was the look about him of a man who is fighting mad—who has been pushed too far and will no longer content himself with merely parrying an opponent's blows. Charlie Mayes saw this. Staring at the flame that glinted in Kincaid's smoldering eyes, the frightened Star boss knew that in the failure of his ambush he had made a fatal mistake. It was death that looked at him from Kincaid's inexorable stare.

"Now get!"

Panic-stricken, Charlie Mayes turned and left that place at a stumbling run. Kincaid watched him out of sight. Then he swung Diablo around and kicked the spurs hard. The murder in his tight-pulled face was a dreadful thing to see.

There was still the sick knotting up of fear inside Charlie Mayes as he tied his lathered horse near a side door at the Leaning 7 house, where a lighted window told him Britt Larkin was likely in the room he called his office. Knowing his way about, Mayes let himself into the house and along the short length of dusky hall to the office door, which stood open. Britt was there, and Jack Beach, who sat with a dusty boot hitched over the arm of one of the heavy, leather-padded chairs. Both were watching the doorway expectantly as the red-haired man entered.

He halted an instant, then went to the desk and sagged against it. "Gimme a drink!" he demanded, and, as Britt Larkin only stared at him, snapped his fingers irritably. "Damn it, I know you got a bottle. Let me have it!"

Larkin's stare, devoid of friendliness, took in the obvious signs of terror stamped in the other man's wild-eyed, grayish features. He leaned and jerked open a drawer of the desk, and lamplight picked out the glint of a bottle and glasses. Before he could lift them out Mayes had reached past him and grabbed the nearly full bottle. He didn't bother with a glass but, dropping into the swivel desk chair, thumbed out the cork and took a long drag directly from the neck of the bottle.

Standing over him, Britt Larkin scowled at his visitor. "So!" he remarked, voicing the thought that had been roweling him for the past hours. "You tried to cut me out! You tried to go behind my back and buy out the Sullivan girl and leave me in the cold with nothing!"

Mayes nearly choked on the fiery liquor. "That's not so!" he blurted hotly, then checked himself as he saw in Larkin's stony face the uselessness of lying. "Kincaid again!" The realization struck home. "He was here! *He* told you!"

"You admit it then?"

"What the hell's the difference now?" Charlie wiped his mouth on the heel of a palm, tossed the bottle onto the desk top. "I'm cleanin' out of this country! Tonight! I come to tell you."

In a stunned silence Larkin exchanged looks with his range boss. "What the devil are you talking about? Where do you think you'll go?"

"I dunno . . . I don't care! Anywhere from here. Kincaid's given me till tomorrow sunup, and I'm takin' it!"

"You mean you'd run from Kincaid? Why, you rotten, yellow——"

Charlie Mayes gripped the arms of the chair, his knuckles white under stretched skin. "Don't!" he gritted. "Don't say it! Because I won't take it off you, Britt! I ain't anyways afraid of you; but Kincaid has sworn to do for me, and I know he can . . . and he will!"

"What's happened?" demanded Larkin, his glance narrowing.

The other told him, then, about the ambush failure. ". . . Butler—killed! . . . Gallen, with a gun arm he'll never use again even if they don't have to saw it off . . . and Blondy Hill . . . Why, they were the best men I had, Britt! But not good enough against Kincaid. He ain't human!"

"Oh, he's human!" muttered Britt Larkin blackly; he was thinking irrelevantly of his wife, with a jealous man's obsession. He felt a stab of doubt that could be shrugged aside only as he remembered that he knew exactly where Irene was just then. She was in her room—he had looked in not ten minutes ago and seen her there, seated before her mirror.

"You think he's human? You'll have a chance to prove

it then!" Mayes let his mouth twist into a mirthless smirk —"because he said to tell you that you were next . . . and he meant it. Once he knows he's rid of me he'll start hunting you, Britt. If you got any sense, you won't wait for it, either!"

"Kincaid's gone crazy!" cried Jack Beach. "I think Sullivan's death has turned him into a madman."

"A damned dangerous one!" Larkin reminded him, and he walked to the window and peered into the gathering dusk, looking at nothing, his face heavy with thought.

Beach stared. "You ain't breakin', chief. You ain't gonna let him scare you out with a couple of words."

His boss turned and looked at him coldly. "I suppose if you were me, you'd like to stand up and trade lead with Kincaid, maybe."

"Well—no," Jack Beach admitted, backing water a little. "I'm glad it ain't me! I ain't his equal with a six-gun. I know that well enough—and there ain't a faster man than me anywhere along the Apache. But there's no need of running, even from Kincaid.

"Between the two outfits, we've got Block S outnumbered four to one. I say wait till dark and hit that place with everything we have. Burn it out. Wipe it clean off the map—and Kincaid with it!"

Larkin shook his head contemptuously. "We'd never get by with such a play! A week ago, yes—our case against Block S was built so strong that nobody would even have lifted an eyebrow. But don't forget it was Port Griswold himself backed Kincaid against you in town today; and since that business of Blondy Hill, Dalhart certainly is in no mood any longer to swallow whatever we tell him. No . . . a raid on Block S is out of the question!"

"Then look, chief!" Jack Beach unhooked his leg from the chair arm, leaned forward. "Give me a little time and the choice of men I need to help me, and——"

"And you'll what? Try another ambush? Or gun him down on the streets of Apache, maybe! And what would Dalhart and the sheriff say to that?" Larkin shook his head. "We can't kill him, and that damned kid, Rooster Adams, blocked our hope of framing him. He's on Block S to stay!"

"Why the hell," Charlie Mayes complained from the depths of bitterness, "couldn't Sullivan have got himself killed just two weeks ago!"

"What you mean is why didn't we do the job for him? We could have, easy—and no kickbacks. But because we thought there was plenty of time, we let it wait while we fell to squabbling over the spoils.

"And now," Larkin finished harshly, "thanks to Kincaid there aren't going to be any spoils. Worse than that! Without the Sullivan grass and water, you realize exactly how much these ranches of ours are worth: nothing! We've ended by losing all the time we put into this proposition!"

Jack Beach opened his mouth to protest . . . then, as the full conviction of what his boss had said struck home, subsided. He looked from one to the other of these men, caught the bad smell of defeat and fear that widened his nostrils, pulled back his upper lip contemptuously.

"Well," he grunted, and started to push himself up from the depths of the chair. "I better tell the boys in the bunkhouse to roll their sougans and come draw their time. Looks like you got no need for a crew after this!"

"Not so fast!"

The tone of Larkin's voice caused the others to look at him sharply. His head was up, his jaw hard with sudden decision. "Maybe," he said slowly, "we did lose out on the main prize, but I ain't leavin' here with nothin'!"

Charlie Mayes demanded, "What do you mean?"

"All those acres down on the Apache, loaded with prime beef . . . and only a short jump through the hills to the border. We know every trail by heart. We've got every herd spotted. Up to now we've done no more than nibble at the edges. But it's all there, waiting—and we've got the men to grab it!"

The immensity of the idea had Charlie Mayes blinking, fighting the fuzziness that liquor had put into his head. "You really think we could? Sweep all those cattle into the hills at one stroke?"

"We ought to get the bulk of them by dividing up the target and picking our shots. Take it roughly by halves: say, you hit the east side with your crew while we go after

Dalhart. There'll be patrols out but not prepared for any-thing on this scale. We can run right over them and be into Mexico by sunrise."

"What becomes of our own beef, here on the bench?"

"A few hundred head of underfed stuff!" Larkin waved them away contemptuously. "Forget them! We won't be coming back here again. Once the drive is safely underway, I'll turn my crew over to Jack while I pick up Irene and some things from the safe I'll be wanting to take along with me; then I'm thumbing my nose at these sun-blasted hills. After this raid, we can set ourselves up as kings down in Mexico."

"Yeah!" The picture was beginning to look good to Charlie Mayes—you could see the greedy anticipation building in his narrow, slanted eyes. "It figures! We got to leave; and we can make it a goin' this valley will never be allowed to forget!"

"And Kincaid?" demanded Jack Beach shrewdly. "You're runnin' away, then, just like he ordered you? You're givin' him this war by default?"

"Why, damn you!" Britt Larkin whirled on his foreman —stung, yet knowing he could not answer because the charge was true. Meaty face ugly, he shouted instead: "You wanted to make a raid tonight; here's your chance at one that will at least pay dividends. You can go along, or back out if you're scared!"

Beach met the angry stare levelly and without hurry eased to his feet. "I don't remember," he observed in an easy tone, "that it was me anybody had accused of being a coward. Sure, I'll go along. But, everything considered, I don't think I'm going to take the risk for no foreman's wages. I suggest we make it a third split."

"A third!" Larkin's throat swelled, angry color leaping into his broad face.

"That's what I said." Beach showed only cool indiffer-ence. "I think you'd need me that much."

It was Charlie Mayes who broke the dangerous dead-lock. "It's O.K. with me, Britt. Jack here knows the trails better than either of us. I reckon he'll earn the difference."

"All right," growled Larkin, his congested blood slowly

receding. "Go on and tell the men what's planning. Any that don't want in on it, I'll pay them off—right now. But I hope you can get them all to stick."

"Oh, I'll get them," promised Jack, and grinned wolf-ishly despite the painful stretching of the lip Ross Kin-caid's fist had swollen for him. "They need any persuading, I can sure as hell do it!"

As he tramped out of the room, heading for the bunk shack, Charlie Mayes got to his feet. The redhead was al-ready nervous with the building of excitement. "I'll get started for my place and alert the boys. We'll be ready to ride with you in an hour."

"In an hour," Larkin nodded, and Mayes was gone.

Britt Larkin, putting a look around him, caught sight of the bottle on the desk. Something made him walk over and pick it up, thumb out the cork, and, after wiping the neck of the bottle on his palm, tilt his head and drink deeply. Lowering the near empty bottle, he gasped and waited for the response of the liquor's fire to hit him.

It came, bringing the hoped-for surge of confidence in tonight's results. Satisfied, he tossed the bottle aside and drew out his six-shooter, proceeded to check the smooth-ness of its action.

XIV   AN OFFER REJECTED

Afterward Irene Larkin came back to her own room and closed the door and leaned all her weight against it. Her breathing was tremulous. She pressed a hand against her heart, lifting the full breast, as though to calm the rapid beating.

She was quite sure she hadn't been detected listening in the hallway outside the office. Nevertheless the flesh of her arms and shoulders was cold, and when she looked into the vanity mirror she saw the pallor of the face reflected there that made the eyes seem larger than they were.

Crossing the room, she looked at herself more closely,

placed both hands against her cheeks to warm them, and stood that way for a moment. Automatically she took up a brush and began dragging it through her thick, dark hair.

She cried out in quick contempt, "The fool!" and slapped the brush down again among the bottles and jars ranged upon the vanity.

Irene had been aware for a long time, of course, of her husband's illicit dealings. There had been no attempt to hide them from her, for Larkin had known that selfish interest would be enough to hold her silent. But surely he didn't imagine now that she would consent to leave this ranch—bleak enough prison as it was—and accompany him into the worse exile of Mexico! And yet, she asked herself bitterly, what else was there for her to do? She had no money—nothing but a few pieces of jewelry that could not last her long. There was money in her husband's office safe, but she had never managed to learn the combination to it. . . .

All at once Irene saw the one possible solution, and she considered it with quickly indrawn breath. It was a risky chance, but she knew her effect on men and specifically she knew what impact their few meetings had made on this Ross Kincaid. It gave her confidence, and with the decision quickly formed she set about at once changing her clothing, dressing for the saddle.

Her prime need now was for haste and, above all, secrecy. Britt was still in his office—she could hear him moving around in there, voicing an occasional exclamation that showed the state of his emotions—but even so there were tense moments before she could close the front door of the house behind her and welcome the deepening shadows of the early night.

The chestnut gelding she usually rode was, fortunately, in its stall at the barn, and so there was not the insoluble problem of trying to rope him out of the night corral. She got the saddle on, working with hurry and constant fear of being discovered by Jack Beach or one of the others, who could likely be depended on to warn her husband even if they did not try themselves to prevent her going.

No incident detained her. Still, she did not breathe

easily until she had led the gelding out of the rear door of the barn and, mounting up, had ridden away from the lamp-dotted buildings at a slow and careful walk. In the line of cottonwoods she halted, turning for a last careful check to determine any sign of alarm. All seemed quiet enough, and she spoke to the gelding and lifted it now to an easy, rolling canter.

But though she had made her departure without challenge and rode now with only the high stars and the gentle desert wind and the drumming of her own mount's hoofs, Irene still knew once or twice a nagging dread of being followed. . . .

Ross Kincaid was walking up to the house from the barn when he caught the first ring of a mount's rhythmic beat coming across the drum of the night-dark earth. He faded back against the corral bars, his gun hand moving by a kind of instinct to check the presence of his belt gun and ease it into the holster. He stood with his fingers touching the butt, head lifted, eyes narrowed as they shuttled back and forth across the night to pick up the first sight of an approaching rider. In the pen at his back, Diablo moved nervously—a blacker shadow against the darkness.

Then the corner of his vision found the vague flicker of movement, and he centered on this and had it clearly pinned as it grew out of the distance and became the pale ghost of a moving horse with a rider—an oddly small shape —clinging to its back. The ranch pup came from nowhere and started a yapping alarm, but Kincaid spoke sharply and brought it whining to heel. Then he was moving forward, calling out, and the horseman veered toward him. A voice called his name: "Kincaid——"

Hoof-raised grit spattered him as the chestnut gelding checked to a halt. He took the cheek strap to settle the mount and hold it at a stand, and looked up in some astonishment at the dimly discernible features of Irene Larkin above him.

He wasn't able entirely to keep this astonishment out of his voice. "What in the world!" he exclaimed. "Is something wrong at your place?"

The woman leaned toward him, placing a hand upon his shoulder. Her hair brushed his cheek, and he felt her breath warm against his face. He slipped an arm about her waist, and she came down from the saddle, her body coming full against him as he lifted her to the ground.

"Ross!" she cried breathlessly. "You must listen to me —and then you must move fast. It's the chance you've waited for; and I've come to give it to you!"

Kincaid still held her in the circle of his arm, the restive mount tugging meanwhile at the fingers he had upon its cheek strap. Both of Irene's hands lay against his chest, and her face was turned up to his, her eyes wells of darkness in the star glow. Something of her excitement was transferred to him as he felt the swelling of her rapid breathing.

"Well?" he demanded.

And in a rush she told him the things she had overheard. She told it all, and he felt something within him turn hard and dark, and somehow evil, at this betrayal.

He would have stopped her rush of words had he known how. He would have refused to listen. But the thing was said, and now she waited for his answer and seemingly knew puzzlement at his continued silence. "Don't you understand?" she cried. Suddenly she had him by the shoulders and was trying to shake him. "Are you listening to me at all—after the risk I ran coming to you—to help you?"

He stood like stone, unyielding to the pressure she put on him. "To help me?" he repeated harshly. "By betraying your husband?" Kincaid had removed his arm from her waist, and now she dropped her hands and stepped back a pace. Her impassioned words broke apart in stammering.

"But I—— You led me to think——"

"I'd say you did the leading," he corrected her coldly. "I went along with the game because . . . well, you're a damnably attractive creature, and a man in my precarious way of life is a fool to pass over his opportunities. I knew, of course, you were selfish—spoiled rotten. I might even have guessed you'd turn against Britt Larkin when you saw his crookedness wouldn't profit you any longer. But that wasn't what I wanted from you!"

Irene sucked in her breath in an audible hiss. Then all at once the dikes broke, and from her lips poured a torrent of abuse—language such as he had never before heard a woman speak. Her hands lifted as though she would strike or claw at him. He merely stood and waited, a little stunned and not at all proud in that moment of the part that he had had in building up to this scene.

And then suddenly she turned to her horse and fumbled for the stirrup. He moved to help her, but she sprang quickly astride, spurning his hand. She took the reins and gave the gelding's head a jerk to dislodge Kincaid's fingers from the cheek strap. From the saddle she looked down at him a long moment, as though she would dredge up further foulness to throw at him.

But she was emptied, and with a jerk of her whole body she reined the gelding about and kicked it forward. Kincaid stared after her with a feeling of something unclean crawling over him. He shrugged this aside, telling himself he was not entirely without blame in this matter.

Because he was what he was, she had come to him with this cheating offer of information to use against her husband. He wished mightily that he could use it, but even to prevent a wholesale raid on the valley ranchers he could not let himself be beholden to Irene Larkin for any favor. . . .

A startled exclamation broke from him. Something was wrong out there in the darkness. Irene's horse had nearly lost itself in the dense shadows, but now he saw it again, growing nearer—heard the quick drum of its hoofs. For some reason Irene was coming back, and he read panic in the way she raced the gelding.

Then behind her Kincaid glimpsed a second rider on a second mount. Quickly this one was overtaking her; now, fifty feet from the place where Kincaid stood, the two figures merged. He heard a man's guttural voice, the woman's frightened scream. They were struggling, the horseman trying to capture Irene's reins or pull her over onto his own saddle.

Kincaid was already running forward, slipping his six-gun from holster. The mounted figures were too occupied to notice him. He came up to them, dodging as one of the horses swerved widely and nearly rammed him. Then he was at the man's stirrup and, reaching, hooked his fingers into the fellow's belt and with a quick haul yanked him out of the saddle.

It was Jack Beach. He landed on his side in the grass and lay motionless, as though stunned, long enough for Kincaid to search for his belt gun and, locating it, pluck it from holster and toss it into the darkness. Irene had quieted her gelding, but he could hear the frightened sobbing of her breath. She said, "He . . . followed me. I almost rode into his hands. . . ."

Kincaid said gruffly, "You're all right. You can go back to your husband."

"To my husband!" she gasped. She pointed at the man in the dirt. "And let *him* tell of my coming here!"

"He'll tell nothing," Ross Kincaid assured her. "Now go on. I'll handle this."

Still she hesitated a moment, as though not yet convinced. But then, without further argument, she pulled away and Kincaid stood listening until he knew that she was safely gone. At last he turned again to Jack Beach, who had pushed to a crouching position and was glaring at his captor and at the six-gun winking starlight in his hand.

"On your feet!" ordered Kincaid.

Sullenly Beach rolled to hands and knees and then to a stand. Head sunk between his massive shoulders, he glared at Kincaid.

He said, "So she told you about tonight."

"What about tonight?" demanded Kincaid, catching him up sharply.

"Nothin'."

But the remark had already sowed its seed. All at once Kincaid knew what he would have to do.

Beach's horse had disappeared into the darkness. Kincaid swung the man around to face the lights of the bunk shack and gave him a prod with the gun barrel. "Start walkin'."

A second nudge convinced him. They went ahead in silence, their boots whispering a ragged rhythm across the dry grass. The ranch pup came up from somewhere and ran silent circles around them.

It was apparent that his encounters with Irene and Jack Beach out at the edge of the dark had caused no disturbance here. Through the bunkhouse window he glimpsed young Rooster Adams scowling over a frayed, paper-backed book. And as they neared the building George suddenly appeared at the barn entrance and with a grunt of surprise came hurrying.

"Get Mac," Kincaid told him briefly. "I want you both."

George, nodding quickly, darted back into the barn again. Kincaid shoved open the door of the bunkhouse and motioned the prisoner through ahead of him.

Rooster looked up—stared; then he came scrambling off the bunk, with his book falling forgotten to the floor. He seemed too astounded to voice a question as Kincaid shoved Jack Beach toward a spur-scarred bench that stood beneath the window.

At about this time they heard George and old Mac approaching at a run; the two hands came bursting in. They looked at the prisoner and at the gun in Kincaid's fist, and old Mac cried, "What in blazes you got here, anyway?"

Kincaid answered: "A gent that figures not to tell me what I want to know. Something's afoot tonight. Before I get through with him I aim to hear from Jack's own mouth just exactly what it is!"

The range boss let his surly stare run across this motley crew and brought it back to Kincaid, with a sneer warping his hard mouth. "You'll scare nothin' out of me! Not you, Kincaid, nor yet this mongrel outfit you ramrod. Not a word!"

This defiance flattened the corners of Kincaid's lips, darkened his eyes. Knuckles whitening on the grip of the six-gun, he said, "You better think again. . . ."

Beach's sneering confidence appeared to crack a little at the edges, but his smoky stare did not waver. "Just go to hell!"

Then an exclamation broke from Rooster Adams. Looking at him, Kincaid saw a strange expression on the youngster's face—a quickening of purpose. "Mac!" the boy grunted; and from his shirt pocket suddenly dragged tobacco sack and papers and thrust them into the old puncher's hands. "Roll me a butt, will you—quick!"

Macready, obviously puzzled but somehow impressed, went to work on it. Rooster looked older than his years just then, and there was a strange intensity in him. It seemed to Kincaid that all at once he could read a sign of apprehension in Jack Beach.

The cigarette made, the tab moistened and pasted down, Rooster held out a hand for it. He had his match ready and in lighting the cigarette got a lungful of smoke that tore a number of painful coughs from him. But he overcame them and, with the glowing butt poised, turned to Jack Beach. Slowly he began moving toward the prisoner.

And the man broke, with a suddenness and completeness that was startling to these others who had no way of understanding the thing they witnessed. "Keep him off!" cried Beach, cringing away from Rooster's approach. "Damn it, Kincaid! I'll tell you! I figure you already know it, anyway. But call that devil off me!"

Kincaid, completely at sea, nevertheless shot Rooster a look that held him. "All right," he told the sweating range boss. "Let's have some talk then. . . ."

The crew was still trying to absorb the meaning of what their ears had heard when Ross Kincaid turned on them to hurl crisp orders. "Get ready to ride . . . in a hurry, with guns and all the ammunition we can scare up! There's no time to waste."

Macready asked, "You think they'll go ahead with their plans even when Beach turns up missing?"

"I'm gambling that way. And it's already too late to try and stop them before they hit the trail down to the valley. . . . Rooster!"

Seeking him out, Kincaid had a new respect for this lad and the baffling way in which he had somehow broken the tough Leaning 7 range boss. Still, any demand for explanations must wait until a better occasion. "Get the horses, Rooster. See if you can find the one Beach rode here and put him in the saddle and tie him good. Our first stop will be at the sheriff's office, to let him repeat his story for Port Griswold."

"Sure, boss! What bronc you aim to ride? Diablo?"

"No—the grulla. That black devil is too gun-shy for what we're likely heading into. Now get going! I have to report to Miss Sullivan. . . ."

He left the bunk shack in a state of high excitement and, crossing the yard to the house, knocked softly on the frame of the screen door. Claire Sullivan as yet knew nothing of what had been happening; busy as usual at her never ending toil, she was clearing the trestle table after the evening meal and in the clink of dirty dishes failed to hear his first rap.

For some reason he held his hand an instant, watching her through the screen—seeing the cool, brisk sureness of bare arms that gleamed in the lamplight, the set of young shoulders, the movement of firm thighs beneath her skirt. Suddenly it occurred to him that there had been a change in her these last days since her father's death. Or, perhaps, the change was in himself; perhaps he had never actually seen her before. . . .

He knocked again and pulled open the screen door as she turned. The sullenness that had been so often in her face was missing now; instead he saw a look of concern, as though she read something in the set of his own features. "What is it?" she demanded breathlessly.

Hat in hand, Kincaid told her. He ended, "We've got to ride, and fast. Will you be afraid to stay here alone, Claire?"

"Of course not," she said quickly. "I have my father's gun, and I can use it if I have to." She added on a note of doubt: "But you—and the men! Must you get into this fight? Isn't it enough if you warn the sheriff and the valley ranchers so that they can protect their own herds?"

"It's not enough," he answered. "I think you see that. The four of us can't affect the outcome much, I reckon; but this is the chance Block S has been waiting for, to show Dalhart and the rest that we're neighbors worth having and respecting. If we pass it up, we may never again have such another."

He started to turn away, the pressure of time riding him hard. But something in her eyes halted him. A golden cross glinted lamplight at her throat; she put a hand up to touch it as she said, in a tone he had never heard her use before, "I'll—be praying for you. . . ."

"For me?" he echoed in numb bewilderment. "I thought you hated me!"

"I hated what I saw in you . . . the hardness, the cynicism. I thought you were a man who hadn't any valid principle or the ability to feel any real human emotion at all."

"And what changed your mind?" His voice was harsh. "When did anything happen to make you think you might have been wrong?"

She said: "I don't know. I think it was the night my father died . . . the way you went out and rode the horse that had killed him—like there was a fury in you. But there was more to it than that. It was a tribute to a man you had respected and—loved. I think you did love my father, Kincaid!"

"Yes." He was a little surprised at his own answer. "Strangely enough, I guess I did. I'd known him just two days, but—well, there was something about him, something different from any other man I'd ever known. . . ."

"It was goodness," Claire replied simply. "Ward Sullivan was a good man, but there had to be goodness in you, as well, to recognize it. That was what I saw. That's what changed my mind!"

"Claire——"

Ross Kincaid blurted her name and then stopped, letting fall the hand he had lifted toward her. And just then, as he groped for words, the voice of Rooster sounded from the night: "Ready to ride, Kincaid? Here's your bronc—and your prisoner!"

The moment broke and crumbled. "Coming!" he answered, turning. He gave Claire Sullivan a brief, last look that etched the image of her in his mind.

Then, dragging on his hat, he strode purposefully to the door, and she stood motionless watching him go. The screen jangled sharply shut behind him.

The jailhouse in Apache was a mere dobe structure twenty feet to a side, housing a single bull pen and a tiny cubicle, where Port Griswold kept his hat and his desk filled with yellowing reward dodgers. It was here that they found the sheriff, and here Jack Beach sullenly repeated his confession, needing no further prodding now that his arrogance and nerve were broken.

Port Griswold heard him through, expressionless, his stare pinned to the man's bruised and sullen face. When the thing was over, the story laid bare, no one spoke for an instant. Port Griswold heaved his ponderous bulk out of his chair, moved heavily to the doorway and stood a moment looking out into the darkness of the plaza. When at last he turned around, he seemed unable to meet anyone's eye directly.

"I'll get my bronc saddled," he mumbled, "and call someone in here to keep guard on the prisoner. Then we'll head fast for Dalhart's. . . ." With a visible effort he brought his glance up from the floor, sought the eyes of each Block S rider in turn. The folds of his throat stirred as he forced the next words out.

"I'm a shamed man! I believed lies, and I hounded an honest gent without quarter and helped make it impossible for Ward Sullivan to build a fresh start. It ain't any good, now, me sayin' I half wished I was dead. . . ."

Embarrassed at the sight of such humiliation, the Block S men could draw little triumph from it. It was Kincaid who spoke, and then only to say, "Maybe we better be trailing. . . ."

John Dalhart had built his ranch on a long slope reaching down toward Apache Creek itself. The ranch house, which utterly dwarfed its entourage of minor buildings, was a glimmering white ghost of a two-storied southern mansion; and on its columned portico Dalhart received these visitors, to listen in unruffled dignity as Port Griswold poured out his startling story.

"Any man can make mistakes," he told Kincaid afterward, "but that makes it no easier to admit them. You'll convey my apologies to Miss Sullivan?" And, satisfied with the other's curt nod, he turned immediately to the issuing of orders, mustering his large bunkhouse crew to meet the threat of raid.

Sheriff Griswold was already lifting his gross bulk again into saddle, groaning heavily. "I got to get warning to the east-valley men," he said.

"Mac! Rooster!" Kincaid ordered. "You go with him. George and I will throw in with Dalhart's crew."

"It isn't necessary," Dalhart told him. "You've done enough already to humble the stiff-necked arrogance of a man who wronged you."

"Nonsense. Those border jumpers have given us trouble, and we want a hand in settling with them—that's all."

"Then you're more than welcome! Come along!"

The main J-D Connected herd, which Dalhart considered surely Britt Larkin's target, grazed on an open, brush-edged flat that could hardly have presented a more enticing picture for a cattle thief. Once get them moving, he pointed out, and the narrowing hills that flanked this valley would funnel them straight southward into broken land and the network of draws and hills beyond which lay the border. Moving in with twenty armed horsemen at their backs, Dalhart and the pair from Block S keened the night anxiously for any mutter of rumbling hoofs that would indicate that they were already too late.

But only the wind in the brush and the creak of their own saddle gear and thud of their horses' hoofs in sear grass disturbed the night's quiet. Reining in finally, they could discern dim shapes of cattle scattered across the black earth before them. "We're in time!" Dalhart muttered, an infinity of relief in his words.

"But just barely," Kincaid warned him. "When they do come, we'll want to meet them at the point of attack and turn it there."

"They'll strike from the north," Dalhart decided. "Just about where we're sitting."

"Then we'll wait for them here. Scatter out. Every man

stay low so we won't be seen until they're right on top of us.
And keep hold of those reins!"

. . . Waiting was the worst part of a business such as
this. Even Kincaid, inured to it by long experience, could
feel a slow crawling of anxiety as he crouched against the
warm earth, the grulla's leathers tied and looped through
his arm, the brush about him rocking in the wind and fan-
ning the bright mesh of the stars.

There was no talk, and throats rough with the need for
smoking had to swallow this hunger, since it had been
strictly forbidden. Kincaid tossed up a pebble and caught it
in his hard palm, over and over. His mind seemed empty
of thinking, drained dry and waiting for the moment of
emergency that would trip the trigger and bring its swift
response.

He almost started when someone spoke his name in a
hoarse whisper. He had so seldom heard the voice of the
man called George that he was slow to recognize it in his
very ear; it was nearly the first time he had ever known the
silent one to venture to speak without being spoken to.
"Kincaid——"

"Yeah?" He kept his answer short and at a whisper;
yet even so it seemed unpleasantly loud in the waiting
quiet.

"There's—one thing I'd like to say," the other faltered.
"It's just that Ward Sullivan was the finest gent I ever
knew . . . the only one who'd hire a man without pryin'
into his past—and without turning nosy afterwards and
driving him off with questions about things that were not
anyone's business.

"I thought a lot of him; and I think a lot of the girl.
I——" He hesitated. "Dunno why I tell you this, except . . .
if anything happens tonight . . . I kind of wish somebody
could know. I waited just too long for Ward to find it out."

Kincaid said, "I reckon I understand." He knew it was
the nearest to a self-revelation he could ever expect from
this strange man of the unexplained past. . . .

Next moment their exchange was fogotten. Kincaid's
head jerked up sharply, and he exclaimed, "Listen!"

"I hear nothing," said John Dalhart; instantly he corrected himself. "Horses! But I can't tell what direction . . ."

With held breath each man studied the sound that had grown now to an audible rumble, which could be felt in the ground beneath them. It didn't come out of the north, where they had looked for it; and, confused, they were for a long, tense moment unable to place its source in the opaque darkness.

Then Ross Kincaid swore and was lunging to his feet. "They crossed us up!" he shouted. "They're hitting straight from the west. They've decided to throw all the beef into one gather and then run it down the center of the valley."

In a mad scramble men threw themselves into saddle. They cursed as their horses circled away at reins' end, sensing the excitement of their owners and nervously trying to evade the hands that grabbed for stirrup iron. But one by one the riders were up and pulling away from that tangle to spur frantically toward the point of threat.

With the wind against his face and slitted eyes, Kincaid heard the first shots somewhere ahead of him; and moments later the grulla's flawless run carried him across a hump, and then he could see the guns winking off there like fireflies. There came the ragged, thin thread of shouts, the bawling of steers in fright, the rumble of the herd breaking into motion. Larkin was risking a runaway stampede in his determination to make a fast job of this—to strike the valley graze hard and sweep it clean in one bold effort.

Then Kincaid and the men of John Dalhart's brand hit those raiders on the flank; and the pattern broke in wild confusion.

Kincaid knew no time, no thoughts. Everything was a welter of dust and earth-shaking sound and streaking powder spark. A moon would have helped, but there was no moon—only the deceptive sheen of starlight, the lifted dust film of sharp, frenzied hoofs. He targeted a mounted figure with a quick shot, heard a human scream that choked off as the rider went down. On every hand, guns were streaking fire in a conflict that hadn't any pattern; and all about were lumbering, frenzied cattle, darting and turning and threatening to rip mounts and men alike with their horns.

He had lost his hat and his long hair was in his eyes and he tossed his head to clear them. One hand held the reins in tight check, the other brandished his smoking gun. A rider moved across his front, but his shot at him missed. Next moment he felt the jar of a bullet that smashed into his metal stirrup guard and ricocheted, narrowly missing disemboweling the grulla.

He triggered again fast, at the same instant roweling the horse cruelly. The grulla buck jumped. It crashed into that other mount, and Kincaid sliced air with his gun barrel. Muzzle flame streaked inches from his face, momentarily blinding him. But the front sight connected solidly, and his opponent went out of saddle. Kincaid lunged ahead.

Above the racket of the guns Larkin's men were shouting back and forth, trying desperately to keep contact in the face of this totally unexpected and demoralizing thrust at their flank. It was, however, increasingly clear that the surprise, and the superiority of numbers in Dalhart's forces, had dealt too strong a blow. There was no holding them. They pushed straight through, hurling back their enemies. And suddenly Kincaid could hear the voice of Britt Larkin himself, cursing insanely in a vain attempt to hold his men together as the fight began to turn into a rout.

Spurring the grulla, Kincaid plunged toward the sound of that voice, and as he went he yelled his enemy's name: "Larkin! Damn you, stand and meet me!"

But the milling pandemonium of bawling steers held him back, though he recklessly dared the clashing horns. And when he had won through, the man he sought was no longer there; the voice had fallen silent. Gun ready, he searched the stinging curtain of dust and smoke but could discover no trace of Larkin.

At the same time he became aware that the shooting had thinned out raggedly, that it was falling off, and that the fight had actually come to an end. He hauled up his sweating mount, trying to order the confused sound and movement.

He could hear the earth-shaking rumble of many hoofs sweeping away toward the east and knew that the herd had been raised into a stampede by the pandemonium of gunplay; but immediately about him was stillness. He drifted on across hoof-torn ground and past the occasional heaped shape of a dead steer or horse. A rider came loping up, and he heard John Dalhart's challenge: "Speak or I fire! Who is it?"

Quickly he declared himself, and they reined their mounts together. "We made a clean sweep of it," Dalhart said, his patrician manners unruffled even in violence. "Larkin's men are scattered and probably on their way to Mexico. I'm willing to let them go if my crew can get these steers gathered and turned before they run off all their tallow!"

"Suit yourself," grunted Kincaid. "Me, I don't figure Britt Larkin should get off that easy. He deserves killing!"

"You think you can catch up with him? The start that he's got?"

"Likely not if he's headed south. Still, I figure there's one stop he'll make before he quits this country." He added, "I can't lose any time. I'll have to leave it to you boys and the sheriff to take care of Charlie Mayes. Larkin's the worst of the pair, and I'm marking him out for my meat. All right?"

"Go ahead!" grunted the rancher. "And luck to you! I'm getting after those cattle—and whatever's going on over at the east end of the valley."

About to rein away, Kincaid turned again for an instant. "One favor, Dalhart. Look out for my crew, will you? George, and Mac, and the Rooster . . . They're good men— all of them. I hope to God they get through this thing whole!"

Dalhart said sharply, "You sound like maybe you didn't expect to!"

Kincaid's shrug was unseen in the darkness. "There's a time for every man. And who knows when it's his number coming up?" With no more than that he had pulled the grulla around toward the western hills and set the spurs.

All was darkness and quiet at Leaning 7 headquarters as Britt Larkin rode in on a flagging, lathered horse. He himself, shaken and unnerved by the disastrous run of the night's doings, had to hang on to stirrup for a moment after dismounting, to let the stiffening return to legs that were rubbery with tiredness and shock.

But there was grim determination in him and the need for haste. He left the sweating horse saddled, on trailing reins, and strode quickly toward the house. The banks of flowers looked dark and unreal in the star shine.

Britt Larkin let himself in through the side entrance and made his way quickly down the hallway's familiar darkness. He knew just where to lay his hand upon matches and the lamp that stood upon the office desk, and in a moment he had a light burning to chase the shadows into the corners of the room

He turned the wick low, not needing much light for what he meant to do; besides, the touch of the lamp glow made him feel somehow uneasy, somehow exposed.

Dismissing this nameless fear, he turned to the box safe and, kneeling, spun the knob and felt the tumblers click into place. The iron door swung open soundlessly. He began taking out packets of green money that he had always kept here in readiness against an emergency such as this . . . and then, suddenly, the yammering insistence of some warning voice within him—telling him that he was not alone in this room—pulled him about, and he saw his wife.

Irene sat in the room's one comfortable chair, in a corner by the window. She was asleep. Her legs were tucked under her, and her head lay back against the cushion in a way that brought out the long, soft line of her throat. With the dark curls against her cheek, and her breast lifting in a slow rhythm to her breathing, she looked very young in the lamplight. Larkin straightened and went over to her, stood a moment looking down at her.

He laid his hand against the soft warmth of her throat.

At the touch she stirred, as a sleeping cat does when it is stroked; then her eyes opened and she was looking up at him calmly and without alarm.

Letting his hand drop to his side, Britt Larkin demanded harshly, "What are you doing here?"

She moved a little in the chair to ease cramped muscles; her eyes, in a cold stare, never left his face. "I had to be sure not to miss you," she answered.

"What do you mean?" snapped Larkin.

"I knew you would be coming." She unfolded herself from the chair, rose, straightening the wrinkles from her skirt with an unconscious gesture. "I knew you'd be after your money—running away and leaving me alone with nothing. I knew you'd forgotten me completely."

The color rose in Larkin's throat. "That ain't true!" he retorted; but, of course, it was. All thought of his wife had slipped from him, and if she had not been here waiting he would have ridden from Leaning 7 without another thought of her—he who had been too jealous ever to let her from his sight. It was a jarring realization, and it made him declare in an even louder voice: "It ain't so, you hear me? Anyhow, why should I be running away? What from?"

"From the man you fear . . . Kincaid!" She spat the name at him.

He struck blindly. The back of his hand hit her mouth, and the unexpected blow drove her into the chair again. She sat there, her eyes glazed briefly with pain. Then fury sparked in them, and her hands gripped the chair arms, pushing her up as she hurled her voice at him. "Yes—afraid! You're a coward, Britt! Coward . . . *coward!*" She fairly screamed the word at him. "And I've lived with you! I've let you touch me . . . loathing you——"

The sudden raging cry that filled Larkin's ears was his own, though he didn't know it. Then he was upon her, and all his frustration poured trembling fury into the big, broad hands that reached and found her throat. Making hoarse, animal noises he shook her like a dog that fastens upon a rabbit; pummeled her head against the back of the chair, his fingers tightening in a sudden wish to destroy the thing that he had loved. She gasped, choking out his name,

pleading. Her fists struck at him, but he did not feel them
or hear her cries, and then strength went out of her blows.

"I'll kill you!" said Larkin through teeth clenched so
tightly that the jaw muscles ached and fluttered. "I'll kill
you sure!"

A crooked arm came from behind then. It took him
about the throat, forced his chin high with a sharp, insist-
ent strength. Suddenly Larkin's hands were torn loose from
their grip, and he went stumbling backward to hurtle
forcibly against the open iron safe. There he half spun,
caught at the object to save himself from falling. And
across his shoulder he saw Kincaid.

The man looked savage and terrible. His face was
pinched down hard in the lamp glow. Dust powdered the
creases of his trail clothing and whitened the tangled hair
that lay against his forehead. He had lost his hat. But his
gun rode its holster, and Britt Larkin felt the danger beating from him like a chilling wind.

Kincaid said, "All right, Britt! It's the end of the line.
You've got enough to answer for without adding murder.
You should be glad I stopped you!"

Their stares met and tangled; and for once Britt Larkin
had no words. He stayed as he was, still clinging to the door
of the safe, still panting, and made no move and no answer.
Then there was a sound from Irene, and Kincaid turned
to her where she crouched in the chair.

Her dress was torn, her dark hair disarranged; her throat
showed the marks of Larkin's throttling hands. She lifted
a hand to her throat and moaned again, and Kincaid put a
glance around the room, looking for whiskey or something
to revive her.

Larkin, watching him, saw instantly that this was the
only chance he would ever have. In his concern for the girl
Kincaid had relaxed caution a moment that could mean
death in a gun duel. Yet, even so, it was only the gravity of
his own situation that gave Britt Larkin the courage to
make his play.

The faint whisper of the gun sliding from leather must
have touched off a warning in the other man. He was half
turned toward the roll-top desk, where he had spotted the

nearly empty whiskey bottle. On the balls of his feet he whirled desperately and stabbed for his own holster gun. And though he had been caught off guard, the speed of his draw once unleashed was a terrific thing.

But Larkin had too strong an advantage, and fear added speed to his arm. Kincaid's gun had not quite cleared leather when the lash of Larkin's weapon smashed upon the room.

The drive of the bullet pushed Kincaid backward against the edge of the doorway and he slid down this to the floor. But the jar of his elbow striking the wall lifted the gun out of leather, and he let this complete the unfinished draw for him; and as he struck the floor he managed to lift the gun and to fire blindly into the echoes of that other shot.

A scream distended Irene's raw throat, and the jarring of this sound across ebbing consciousness opened Kincaid's eyes, which smarted with the sting of powder stench. Through a reddish haze he looked around him, wondering at the odd angle of things before realizing that he was still* sitting in a sprawl against the doorjamb.

He thought of rising, changed his mind. There was a leaden weight of inert deadness somewhere in his middle body, with red pain shot through it. He saw the blood already soaking through his clothes when he craned to peer down at himself. He couldn't tell just where Larkin's bullet had entered, but he supposed he must be gut shot.

He had seen men die that way; he knew it would be horrible.

He heard a voice croaking, "Whiskey!" and realized it was his own. Yonder, Britt Larkin lay in a sprawl of unmistakable death. Loose green money had spilled from a side pocket of his coat as he fell, and it lay all around him, and some had Larkin's blood on it.

Then Irene was kneeling beside Kincaid, making incoherent outcries, her hands touching him but without competence, without knowledge of what she could do to help him. This angered Kincaid, and he snarled at her, "Whiskey, damn it!" He would need all the fortification he could get against the thing that he knew lay ahead.

But she did not move to get the bottle; merely hovered

helplessly beside him in that same unavailing solicitude, saying his name over and over. The very sight of her irritated him, and he felt his lip curl, felt his face stiffen into a mask of contempt that perhaps was worse than this woman deserved from him; but he could not now be concerned over the justice of his treatment of her.

"You got the wrong man," he told her harshly. "That's your husband. He'll be no more use or no more harm to you. The ranch is yours—though, more likely, the money on the floor is what you'll want, to take you as far from this land as you can get. There's blood on it . . but that shouldn't bother you any!"

He didn't care how the cruel speech hurt her. He figured he was too close to death for anything but the truth to interest him. Her face seemed to blur before his eyes, then take on hardness and malevolence. And he remembered one more thing that he must make clear to her and roused himself to the effort of framing speech:

"I just wanted you to know . . . it's no credit to you that we cut in on that raid tonight. I got the whole story out of Jack Beach before I'd act on it. I wouldn't let myself be owing to you for anything."

She slapped him— hard . . . so hard that his swaying head was knocked back against the wall and then fell forward again, too heavy for his strength to hold it up. But he scarcely felt the blow. The pain in his belly was widening, spreading, blooming like a fiery flower. He could not move, could not even think clearly.

His last concrete thought was that Irene Larkin, wherever she might go now or whatever she might do with the dubious legacy her husband had left her, was no problem of his or of Claire Sullivan's. No, neither she nor anyone else could harm Block S now. And he was glad, if this had to be the end of his long and dubious trail, that he'd at least been able to finish the job for the Sullivan girl.

Only, it was too bad really. He had found something on that hard-pushed hill ranch—something he had missed before in all his years on the go . . . something he would have liked to keep. At first he hadn't liked this border country. But if he had lived, he thought he would like to

have stayed on awhile and end his roving. Work for Claire
Sullivan, at ordinary foreman's wages. If he had lived . . .

He did not know when hoofs broke the silence of the
ranch yard and boots came clomping into the hallway. He
did not hear Macready's anxious cry of "Here he is—and
murdered!" or feel the roughly gentle hands that lifted and
carried him out into the early dawn. He did not know the
jolting of the buckboard that took him away from that
deserted place, or anything of the careful ride to Block S.

But then he was in Ward Sullivan's bed, in the familiar
room of the humble ranch house. There were the faces of
the crew. Dazedly he counted them, two times over, con-
vincing himself finally that they had all come through
the ordeal of that night of battle virtually unharmed
except for the bullet-broken arm whose bandage young
Rooster Adams wore proudly as the badge of his initiation
to gunfire. The battle had ended in a triumph, they said.
Though no one knew for sure whose bullet it was that
actually took the life of Charlie Mayes. . . .

Later there was the doctor—a tobacco-stained character,
who shook his head and muttered: "I just don't get it at
all! He should be dead, the way that bullet plowed through
him. And yet I declare he's going to mend! It's enough to
make an old sinner believe in miracles. . . ."

There was Claire's whisper, warm against his ear as she
kneeled beside him: "I prayed for you . . . I prayed every
minute that you'd come back to me."

And suddenly there came a memory of his own harsh
and knowingly cynical words: "When I see a miracle—
when I see a dead man walk—then maybe I'll believe. . . ."
And, remembering, he knew he had had his answer.

He reached, trembling, and touched the girl. At once
Claire Sullivan moved into the circle of his arm. Her lips
were soft upon his own; her breath touched his face. Kincaid accepted all that had been granted him, in a humble
gratitude.

Dwight Bennett Newton is the author of a number of notable Western novels. Born in Kansas City, Missouri, Newton went on to complete work for a Master's degree in history at the University of Missouri. From the time he first discovered Max Brand Street and Smith's *Western Story Magazine*, he knew he wanted to be an author of Western fiction. He began contributing Western stories and novelettes to the Red Circle group of Western Pulp magazines published by Newstand in the late 1930s. During the Second World War, Newton served in the U.S. Army Engineers and fell in love with the central Oregon region when stationed there. He would later become a permanent resident of that state and Oregon frequently serves as the locale for many of his finest novels. As a client of the August Lenniger Literary Agency, Newton found that every time he switched publishers he was given a different byline by his agent. This complicated his visibility. Yet in notable novels from *Range Boss* (1949), the first original novel ever published in a modern paperback edition, through his impressive list of titles for the Double D series from Doubleday. *The Oregon Rifles, Crooked River Canyon*, and *Disaster Creek* among them, he produced a very special kind of Western story. What makes it so special is the combination of characters who seem real and about whom a reader comes to care a great deal and Newton's fundamental humanity, his realisation early on (perhaps because of his study of history) that little that happened in the West was ever simple but rather made desperately complicated through the conjunction of numerous opposed forces working at cross purposes. Yet through all of the turmoil on the frontier, a basic human decency did emerge. It was this which made the American frontier experience so profoundly unique and which produced many of the remarkable human beings to be found in the world of Newton's Western fiction.